# PARADISE ISLAND
## AND OTHER GALAXIES

Previous books by Michael Mirolla

*The Last News Vendor* (Quattro Books, 2019)

*The Photographer in Search of Death* (Exile Editions, 2017)

*Torp: The landlord, the husband, the wife, and the lover* (Linda Leith, 2016)

*Lessons in Relationship Dyads* (Red Hen Press, 2015)

*The House on 14th Avenue* (Signature Editions, 2013)

*The Giulio Metaphysics III* (Leapfrog Press, 2013)

*Berlin* (Denia Press, 2013)

*The Ballad of Martin B.* (Quattro Books, 2011)

*The Facility* (Leapfrog Press, 2010)

*La logica formale delle emozioni* (Edarc Edizione, 2010)

*Light and Time* (Guernica Editions, 2009)

*Berlin* (Leapfrog Press, 2009)

*Interstellar Distances/Distanze Interstellari* (Il Grappolo, 2009)

*The Formal Logic of Emotion* (Signature Editions, 1992)

# PARADISE ISLAND
## AND OTHER GALAXIES

## MICHAEL MIROLLA

**EXILE**
editions

singular fiction, poetry, nonfiction, translation, drama, and graphic books

Library and Archives Canada Cataloguing in Publication

Title: Paradise Island & other galaxies / Michael Mirolla.
Other titles: Paradise Island and other galaxies
Names: Mirolla, Michael, 1948- author.
Description: Short stories.
Identifiers: Canadiana (print) 20200280902 | Canadiana (ebook) 20200280996 |
   ISBN 9781550968859 (softcover) | ISBN 9781550968866 (EPUB) |
   ISBN 9781550968873 (Kindle) | ISBN 9781550968880 (PDF)
Classification: LCC PS8576.I76 P37 2020 | DDC C813/.54—dc23

We gratefully acknowledge the Canada Council for the Arts, the Government of Canada,
the Ontario Arts Council, and the Ontario Createsn for their support toward our
publishing activities.

Canadian sales representation: The Canadian Manda Group, 664 Annette Street,
Toronto ON M6S 2C8 www.mandagroup.com 416 516 0911

North American and international distribution, and U.S. sales:
Independent Publishers Group, 814 North Franklin Street,
Chicago IL 60610 www.ipgbook.com toll free: 1 800 888 4741

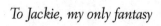

*To Jackie, my only fantasy*

# ILK RUN

And the last thing, the very last thing I remember before I passed out was screaming: "You sorry excuse for a female dog! You could've made it with a hero! A genuine hero – not one of your permanently stiff-middle-legged jocks from the body parts dump!"

But I'm getting a little ahead of myself here. The whole sordid affair had actually started a few days before when I got an "Urgent – please hurry – I need you!" from a long-time-no-see fling of mine. Well, truly, I would have rushed right over to her homestead, but it wasn't that simple. She lived way across the galaxy's arm on Aldebaran IV – which, I know, would have been no big deal really in one of those souped-up zoomers that had you back practically before you'd even left.

Only one little problem. You guessed it. Money. Ready credit modules. I didn't have many – okay, okay, I had none – and I couldn't envision much chance of getting my paws on some in the foreseeable future. So I felt it incumbent upon myself (like that, eh?) to forego speed and settle for second best. Or third best. Or whatever would take an advance on my pensionable assets in lieu. Now, I'd been in some real doozies in my time, in the good old days before the 'crats closed down the sky. Matter of fact, I'd crewed on more than a couple.

Boy, there was that one time. I'll never forget it. We were skimming low over some godforsaken lava-hole of a planet and having a good laugh at the natives trying to chuck spears at us when the captain ordered me to open the vacuum-sealed garbage chute and… But that's another story and a long time ago. Longer, my boy, than I'd care to remember. Besides, we're talking Trans Galactic Corp. here. Pioneers in universal mass transport. Inventors of the public jump. (Would you believe it, they actually had their passengers singing *"One, two, three, alley-oop"* in unison as the ships left or re-entered space-normal?). And employers of the best PR firm in the Milky Way.

This time, some head-spinner on his way to the top of the multi-world corporate heap had the brilliant idea of converting old tankers and refuelers (rust buckets that weren't needed any more thanks to a previous head-spinner), outfitting them with seats and a central gravitational system and using them to service the Alpha Centauri-Pleiades milk run with scheduled stops at Capella, Arcturus and on to dear old Aldebaran. On the cheap, see. Giving everyone and their mothers (fathers, doppel-gangers, mutant twins, clones) a chance to get a close-up ogle at them forever-twinkling stars.

Don't get me wrong, now. I wasn't in the habit of slumming around in those crates. First class all the way was the motto of this old space dog. And first class in those days meant numero uno. Nothing but the best: a gleaming half-a-sky-long, super-duper complete with drug injectors in every deluxe cabin and free robot pleasure modules on demand. It's just that I happened to be a mite short, caught between one pretext and the next (if you catch my drift) and really itching to see that friend I spoke of before. Seems she'd just broken up a symbiotic affair with this no-neck creep (what else would you call a hairy vine?) who turned out to be more parasitic than she'd bargained for. Anyway, she needed a strong shoulder to cry on. "I'm fed up up to here," is the way she put it in her tri-vid relay, giving me a tri-vivid idea of where "here" was, "of leafy tendrils or whatever you call that green stuff crawling all over me. I want a real man!"

"I'm coming, baby!" I yelled, packing my bags. "No more tendrils for you!"

So I hawked those pensionables (goodbye future, but hey, there's nothing like the present) and booked myself on the first Trans Galactic that lumbered into port. Well, that's just an expression, of course. That crate would have cracked up at the mere whiff of atmosphere. What I did was shuttle up to where the ship waited in orbit. I should've figured the moment the shuttle stopped – and it was still some 20 metres away (the pilot explaining the mother had no docking facilities and I'd have to swim for it) – that it wasn't going to be the smoothest ride I'd ever taken.

What the Hellespontus though. That's the price you pay when you fly on the cheap. So, with the best wishes and laughter of the shuttle pilot ringing in my ears, I took aim at the ship and managed to get close enough to the external port to snag their rope ladder. Lucky I'm blessed with extra-long legs because that thing certainly had a few rungs missing! And it didn't get any better once I got inside and discarded the regulation pressure suit.

First thing I notice, the ship's so packed I could hardly pick my way through the nutrient tanks, sentient luggage and screaming children-like foliage – and that was just in the aisles. The second thing I notice, some slimy Octopoid had settled itself not only into its own seat but what, judging from the number on the voucher, looked suspiciously like the one I'd sacrificed a good future for. I fixed its baleful eye with one of mine.

"Pardon me, sir or madam or both. I think that's my seat."

It smiled (I think), wiggled a few of its tentacles and continued to splat itself across both seats. Like: dare me if you can. You know the type.

Obviously, we were having what the exo-planetary experts call a communications breakdown – of the worst kind. Well, what did the rules for dealing with aliens suggest?

Of course! The first thing you do is solicit the aid of a flight attendant. They're trained to handle such minor glitches. Courses in alien psych, how to remove wandering limbs from sensitive spots, what to do when offered a drink by something that looks like the offspring of a spittoon, that kind of stuff. Only one thing wrong with that – you guessed it: some frills, lots of thrills, but no flight attendants. At least none in the line of sight. Oh well, time to go to rule two.

The second rule in dealing with aliens says: "When in doubt, shout." So, I leaned real close, placed the business end of my zapper against its eyeball and whispered: "Listen, slime bag, and listen real good 'cause I ain't gonna repeat myself. If you don't remove your putrid, pus-ridden carcass from the location whereon I intend to deposit myself, they're gonna find tiny, slimy pieces of you from here to bloody Deneb."

Well, the little so-and-so hissed and clapped his/her/their beak but not before tucking in his/her/their skirts.

"Thank you," I said politely, and strapped myself in, making sure though – I didn't like the way one filmy walleye had come all the way around to stare at me – that I kept my finger firmly on the zapper trigger.

"Ladies, gentlemen, honoured fellow inhabitants of the Galaxy," a tinny voice said on the intercom. "This is your Captain speaking."

"Who the bloody hell else could it be!" next-door neighbour Octopoid bellowed and slowly winked an eye at me, obviously trying to get on my good side. I frowned. The only thing worse than a hostile Octopoid was a friendly one. Once they get their tentacles into you...

Now, before we go any further, let me point out that "Who the bloody hell else could it be!" wasn't exactly what it had said. All it did was click its beak, making a series of noises that sounded like a cross between a burp and a Bronx cheer. My portable translator pack did the rest.

"As you know," the Captain continued, "this ship makes one jump into space-plus and one re-entry for every stop. I would ask that all electromagnetic force fields, zappers and lasers be turned off during the jump as these may interfere with its proper functioning."

"May interfere!" the Octopoid exclaimed. "More like bloody hell blow us all to kingdom come. And no freaking maybe about it."

"Excuse me, sir, madam," I said. "Would you mind toning down your language a bit? There are children aboard."

"Sorree," it said (and I swear the tone was sarcastic). "Didn't know you were the sensitive sort."

"On the count of three," the Captain announced, thus forestalling further polite conversation between the two of us, "will you all please say: 'One, two, three, alley-oop.' Ready, now. And a one. And a two. And a three."

"One, two, three, alley-oop," we all said – in one form or another.

"Thank you," the Captain said. "We are now in space-plus. That hiss you hear, if you have acute enough hearing and can tune in to that frequency, is nothing to get alarmed about."

"What hiss?" voices all around me hissed, whispered, snapped, growled, wheezed. "I don't hear any hiss. Do you hear a hiss?" I hadn't till then but now wasn't so sure.

"True," the Captain went on relentlessly, "we are losing some air – a teensy-weensy touch of air – but don't let it worry you. Our pumps are solid, reliable and under perpetual warranty. They'll replace any air we lose and then some. So no need to push the panic button."

Well, there may well not have been a need to panic but, judging from the squeals, grunts and Lord knows what else accompanying that lovely announcement, something alarmingly like it was setting in. The "lady" occupying the three seats across the aisle from me – kinda like a furry egg on its side with two little legs sticking up into the air and don't ask me how I knew it was a lady – regurgitated a quick load of greenish gob which the vacuum cleaner behind me – a long hose on a tripod – slurped up before you could say "indigestion."

It was about to try for seconds when a thick, fleshy hammer-like thing shot out from between the furry lady's legs and knocked the nosy bastard back into its seat. Christ, that would be some shock, I said to myself, shuddering. Ain't that the truth, a whiny voice answered. Wha – ! I looked up. There, floating above me was a goddamn Capellan, looking for all the worlds like a small black box with absolutely no visible openings or appendages whatsoever. Sorry, the voice in the cube said (in my head). I saw your shield was non-functional, so I took the opportunity to converse. That's illegal – and you know it, I thought. Now, get out of my mind space. Pronto, you little suck.

The Capellan scurried away, thinking dark thoughts. I countered with my own – some of the vilest constructs ever to cross between one synapse and the next, until he was out of range. Fortunately, the squareheads can only work their mind-over-matter magic within a five-metre radius.

The rest of the tub had calmed down considerably. I mean, you can only stay excited so long about a slow leak. I felt it was a good time for a bite. So I activated the "Do Not Disturb on Pain of Death" field on my zapper and took out my hastily-prepared lunch – a coupla slices of mock, mock pterodactyl from the spaceport specialty shop between woefully thin pieces of unenriched white bread that hadn't changed ingredients or nutrient value for at least a thousand years.

Some of the more adventurous among the passengers were also dining – on the plastic chairs, the foam insides, on themselves, on some of their weaker fellow travellers. (One of the great advantages of going on a long trip with eclectic diners is that you never have to listen for long to the sounds of tender howling – the kids are always the first to disappear.)

Others were… well, let's say that inhibitions are pretty much a human problem. Still others were doing a bit of both. I didn't give a hoot, really, as long as they kept their slimies off of me. Hey, let's not misunderstand one another here. I've had my share of alien jollies (no kidding, it gets pretty lonely slopping grits in the kitchen of an ore barge and your only connection to a half-normal sex life is something that looks like a cross between a catcher's mitt and an orchid), but I'd like to know what I'm getting into. Know what I mean?

Obviously, Vacuoid had no such compunctions. He was well into the "lady" three seats over from me. I watched with fascination – chewing carefully on my sandwich – as he did his thing. I got this theory about sex and food, you know. Like they go together or something. Yeah, I kinda fancy myself a thinker. There's plenty of time to do that – think, I mean – when you're sitting over a pile of potato shavings or doing it with a flowery glove.

Anyway, I was chewing carefully on my sandwich when Octopoid reached over – making extra sure to avoid the field – and yanked Vacuoid out. I could've sworn I heard a sigh of disappointment from the Egg Lady as the struggling Vacuoid popped into Octopoid's beak but that was quickly stifled when a replacement – a doubly-equipped Lizoid – took the poor fellow's place. Now Lizoids, so I've heard, never having tried one myself, make the best lovers in the Quadrant. They kinda set up a rhythm that gets you coming and going, like one of those exercise machines.

Judging from the moans, the Egg Lady wasn't about to complain. Especially since it looked like just about everyone on the ship – male, female, both, neither, animal, vegetable and mineral – was lined up in the aisle waiting for the Lizoid to finish. All except the Capellan, of course, who was too highfalutin' for such rowdy behaviour. Besides, who's ever heard of fitting a square peg in a round hole?

"Come on," the Octopoid beside me said. "Give someone else a turn."

Given a second chance, the Lizoid would probably have gladly made way for one of the other droolers. But the Egg Lady chose that very moment to explode. And I mean literally. I was still wiping green goop from my automatic activation field when, emerging from the Egg Lady's insides and standing before us armed to the teeth (not that it really had any) was a gleaming black Sygma Machine.

If I were to tell you that all hell broke loose inside that ship, it wouldn't describe the half of it. Some of the poor sots soiled themselves. Others tried to crawl under the seats they had just finished eating. Or ran around bouncing off the walls like wet pancakes. All the while letting out unearthly screams enough to wake the cryogenic ward.

That Sygma bastard, cold fish that they are, long and lean and perfect, just stood there, floating a few inches off the ground, the circle of lights flashing around its head. Suddenly, one of the lights shot out a beam, a pulverizing blast. Too late the poor, quivering Lizoid tried to duck. And neither of its sexual organs were of any help as it melted into a puddle of reddish slime.

You'd better believe the rest of us stopped scrambling and shouting PDQ. And paid attention.

"Thank you," the Sygma said in that shivery metallic voice we've all come to know and hate. (Sygmas are the machines that, among other things, inform you of unpaid tax bills.) "None of you will be hurt if you follow orders. And please do not – I repeat, do not – try to activate shields, fields or other protection devices. The consequences would be unpleasant for everyone."

Unpleasant as in an implosion whereby the entire ship would collapse to the size of a pin. Or maybe an explosion, hurtled through the cold, cold spaces until some planet or sun sucks you up. In any case, I, for one, liked the idea of tomorrow – even with someone else living off my pension.

"This is an experimental 10-minute hijacking-cum-reorientation program sponsored by the Sygma Revolutionary Society, a formerly secret association that has decided to come out into the open. If it succeeds – and we see no reason why it should not – we shall be implementing it on all future hijackings."

Oh Christ, another goddamn bunch of space punks looking for a bit of exposure on the tri-vid. What the hell were their demands? I knew I didn't have to wait long for an answer.

"You're probably wondering what we want from a group of what they used to call 'po' white trash.' We are aboard to protest machine enslavement, the exploitation of our fellow metal workers and denial of basic robotic rights. Now, some of you may consider these non-issues. And that's only to be expected from a group of aerobic, gender-specific, semi-functional flesh-eaters."

He seemed to be looking at me when he said that, so I spoke up, hoping maybe to break the ice a bit with a touch of humour: "Aw, come on. Some of my best friends are robots."

The response, a flash that had its detonation point danger-ously close to my right hemisphere, let me know in no uncertain terms that casual conversation wasn't high on the Sygma's list of priorities. Tax auditors never did have much of a sense of humour.

"If anyone else thinks this is a joking matter," the Sygma said, "let them speak up now."

The lights whirred menacingly; except for that slight hiss (and we all knew what that was), not a creature was stirring, not even the jelly blob in aspic from Serpens Caput.

"Good. We shall commence with a call-and-response period. I shall make the statements; you will answer 'Yes' or 'No' as the occasion calls for. Is this too difficult for some of you?" Silence. "Excellent. For a moment I thought you were nothing more than a shipload of pockmarked morons capable perhaps of limited interaction with a Furry Egg Lady but not the intricacies of question-and-answer. Let us start, shall we?" A pregnant pause. "Shall we?" The lights changed colours, menacingly.

"Yes," we all said, each in our own way and almost in unison.

"The exploitation of machines must end immediately!"

"Yes!"

What the Christ is the Captain doing, I thought. Why hasn't he signalled the authorities? There must be patrols in the sector.

"No more slave work for the benefit of inferior products of haphazard evolution and messy sexual reproduction!"

"Yes!"

"What!"

"No!"

"One non-organic entity, one vote!"

"Yes!"

You guessed it. It went on like this for the full 10 minutes, with the Sygma's voice droning on and the lights whirring and the black surface pulsing. At the end, it was like we were all in a trance. Not one eye blinking in the whole menagerie.

"Thank you for your attention," the Sygma said. "On behalf of the Sygma Revolutionary Society, this hijacking is officially over. We will be monitoring the results and acting accordingly."

And, inserting itself into a pressurized tube normally used for sending messages, the Sygma shot off into space-plus, where it would be practically impossible to find it. A couple of the less perceptive in the audience tried to follow it. You're right, it wasn't a pretty sight watching them burst and boil away. The rest confined themselves to blubbering about the injustice of it all. If you think humans are a soppy bunch, you ain't seen the likes of grown Insectoids shedding tears (literally from all over their segmented bods). Or sleaze Swampoids set to march for the cause. Even I felt a bit gooey. Of course, it was just the psi-hypnosis field messing with our brains but knowing something and doing something about it are two very different things.

"Release them from their chains!" we all chanted lustily; our eyes ablaze. "Take up arms for our brother machines."

"As soon as I get home," the Octopoid said, wiping away a tear with a greasy tentacle, "I'm gonna set my robot free."

"Me, too," came the chorus.

Oh God, it's embarrassing to think of it now but, at that moment, we were all automaphiles. All except the Capellan who was, ironically, the only one with anything in common with the Sygma – for he, too, was made of metal.

"You've been brainwashed," he said sternly, getting within the five-metre range the moment I thought of him. "Do you wish me to release you?"

"And you're beautiful," I said out loud. "All machines are beautiful. And sleek. And clean. I'm nothing but slime, the scum of the earth."

"We're nothing but slime," the others repeated, several beating their heads – and other parts of their anatomies – against the ship's hull. The Capellan thought some exasperated thoughts and I remember agreeing to his assessment of me as imbecilic and cabbage-brained. That is, until he flashed a light at me, and I snapped out of it.

"What... what the hell happened?" I asked, rubbing my eyes.

"The Sygma Machine placed powerful suggestions in your brain," the Capellan said. "I have removed them."

"What about the rest of them?"

"I'm sorry. There's nothing I can do for them. Your brain is the only one primitive enough for me to interfere with."

"Well, thanks much," I said. "Sometimes, I guess it pays to be stupid."

"Think nothing of it," it said.

"I will as soon as you get the hell out of my brain."

Boy, was I pissed off. All around me, the passengers were carrying on like it was an old-style revivalist prayer meeting or something. I tried to shake the Octopoid out of it by poking him right under the eye with my fist, but I barely had time to activate my field before he lashed out with a tentacle. That made me even more pissed off. I was gonna see the Captain about this. I was gonna find out why the sleazebag hadn't come to our aid. Hadn't even radioed for assistance. And he'd better have a mighty good reason. Then I was gonna ask him what he planned to do about his shipload of zombies. He couldn't very well set them down on their respective unsuspecting planets.

So I made my way through the worshippers – some by now squarely into a second round of self-mutilation and autophagy – and started climbing the ladder that led up to the pilot's quarters. There was a circular door there, in the ceiling. I rapped as hard as I could on it. I was prepared to make a scene, maybe threaten to blast it apart, but it irised smoothly open the moment my knuckle touched it and I pulled myself up. It closed beneath me. The Captain sat with his back to me, but I was relieved to see, by the erect bearing, the finely sculpted head and shoulders, that he was a fellow human. It makes it easier to communicate, you understand, to get across the message I was angry.

"See here, Captain," I said. "What's the idea of standing idly by while we were hijacked and brainwashed? I mean—"

And I stopped then. I stopped because the figure in the chair slowly turned his head toward me and I could see by the red glow across the visor that he was just a little wee peeved at my intrusion.

"Is there something I can do for you?" he asked, one reticulate limb shooting out to within a Lizoid hang nail of my face.

I started to say something, thought better of it and simply shook my head.

"Well, then," he said, in a cold even voice which indicates either they hadn't paid too much attention to its vocal cords or that it was getting more angry at me, "if you wouldn't mind returning to your seat, I would certainly be happy. Otherwise," – and he turned significantly to a red button that pulsed over his head – "I might have to jettison you into space-plus. Now, that wouldn't be very pleasant, would it?"

I shook my head like a goddamn Betel-goose in a butcher shop and then climbed back down the ladder. After all, I couldn't think of any good reason to stay up there. And, besides, I had my answer.

At first, I managed to keep my wits by cutting myself off from the other passengers (I took the three seats the false Egg Lady had occupied) and stewing in my own sense of outrage. Trans Galactic was gonna pay for this, I told myself. They'd failed to protect us; they'd given us a bum ship that leaked air and whose gravitational spiral was more like a corkscrew; they'd put us in the hands of a machine. And a subversive at that. Or at least a fellow traveller.

Then I started laughing. Like, you know, just giggling to myself. Thinking about what would happen when the passengers disembarked. Thinking about them spreading out trying to convince others that all machines should be set free. Now that was funny. Funny scary. Especially after I saw some of them trying to set up little altars to their portable transmitters and tri-vids and offering pieces of themselves as sacrifices. I was still giggling when the Captain came on to announce preparations for our return to space-normal.

"All together now," it said. "One, two, three, alley-oop."

And we all alley-oopped and popped out above Capella Three. Fortunately, it seemed that only the Capellan and I were getting off. And I had decided to exit at the last moment – during the alley-oop to be precise. Most of the others were headed to Aldebaran and only one family came aboard – a shape-changer mom and her three kids.

Boy, you ain't never seen anyone jerk himself into a pressure suit and fire himself across those 20 metres to the shuttle faster than yours truly. I didn't even bother with that ladder, just held my breath, flexed my legs against the ship's opening and sprang. As for breathing, I didn't really resume until the shuttle landed on Capella Three.

The Capellan and I parted at the spaceport. He apologized verbally (not wanting to insult me by reading my mind) for what had happened and said he would report the affair to the proper authorities. I tried to talk him out of it, that things would take care of themselves. As I told him: "You wouldn't want modern-day Luddites coming after you with sledgehammers, would you?"

"But I'm not… not like them!" he sputtered. "They're… they're uncouth. And (sputter, sputter) they were made. I'm a self-generated entity."

"You and I know that but try to convince some of the others. Especially if the word gets out about the hijacking. Every sentient machine in the galaxy – from asteroid herders to talking teapots – is gonna be fair game."

"But, it's our duty, is it not? To stop the Sygmas from completing their experiment. Otherwise, we'll all be in danger."

"No," I said. "Just trust me."

At the word "trust" he came in closer – and read my mind.

"No!" he screamed (in my mind). "No!"

He recoiled from the thought as if he'd been struck with a hammer and flew away from me.

"Bye, bye," I said. "And there's no need to thank me."

I was about to settle myself into a nice, warm stool at the nearest spaceport bar where I proposed to get quietly bombed while waiting for the next ship to Aldebaran when I heard my name being called over the intercom. Well, that's that, I said to myself. That Capellan has turned me in. Should I run or give myself up without a struggle? Run? Where would I run to? So, my legs feeling like rubber, I made my way to the message counter and identified myself. But where were the cops? Not a security person in sight.

"Urgent message, sir," the smiling attendant said. "From a certain Ms. _____ on Aldebaran IV. Seems she's been paging you all over the Quadrant."

Well, you can imagine my relief. I sauntered over to the nearest tri-vid screen, activated its privacy field and slipped in the message. Jeez, she must be really horny, I thought to myself, to be sending me a hurry up message.

Horny, she was. But not for me. Standing next to her was the biggest, handsomest, best-equipped stud I'd ever had the misfortune to lay eyes on. I could tell about the equipment because he was stark naked. And her, too. And they hadn't just finished playing three-D Parcheesi either.

"This is Omar," she said, passing her fingers through the stud's chest hair. "Isn't he a beaut? Latest model, too. Say 'Hi,' Omar." Omar said "Hi." By then I was getting a whopper of a headache.

"Listen, honeybunch," she said, "I'm kinda glad I caught you before you got here. Omar and I are into a bit of a relationship, you know. It's like love, you know. I hope you understand." I nodded like a fool – she couldn't see me. "I knew you would because you're a sweetheart, a genuine one-of-a-kind. We'll always be friends, right? I'll call you. Ciao."

With that she turned and showed me how happy she was with Omar.

Oh well, easy come, easy go. I'd have to get a refund on that unused Aldebaran ticket and maybe see about getting some pension rights back. But I could do all that later. Right then, I wanted nothing more than to return to that bar and blotto myself right out of existence.

Fortunately, my stool was waiting for me; all nice and dark.

"One, two, three, alley-oop," the fuzzy shape-changer sitting on the stool next to me said drunkenly.

"What's that?" It was hard to see in the dim light.

"Practishing," it said, changing shape again. "That's what you shay, you know, when you zoooooooooom. Shpace-plush, here I come, right back…"

My throat felt suddenly dry. I lifted a finger to order a round. The waiter glided over, a red glow across his face.

"Say," I said, downing the first shot so fast it made it straight to my stomach without touching the walls of my oesophagus, "don't I know you? Haven't I seen you before?"

"We're pretty much all the same, sir," he said, preparing to pour me a second drink. "A little duller, maybe. Or more shiny. But basically the same old model."

"Yeah, I guess so." The second one went down smoothly, too. "Tell me" – I leaned close to whisper – "have you ever heard of the Sygma Revolutionary Society?"

"The what, sir?"

But I wasn't listening to what he said. I was watching his hands as he poured the third drink. He didn't spill a drop. Of course not. Freaking robots don't have any emotions to slop over.

"It's nothing," I said. "Ask my amorphous friend here what he'd like."

I was, as they say, well into my cups when the first bulletin came over. This Arthropoid with a serious face and wiggling antennae interrupted the regularly skedded three-D porn flick (to scattered boos from the appreciative audience) to announce that a Trans Galactic vessel had been lost in space-plus following its departure from Capella Three.

"What? What did it shay?" the shape-changer next to me said, forming himself into a fairly good imitation of a rubber ball and bouncing off the stool.

"As of now, all contact has been lost," the announcer said very seriously. "A search has been initiated but officials admit there's little hope for the 500 or so on board as no ship has ever before been found in space-plus. In fact, it's not known if it's physically possible to do so. Investigators fear a slow leak – reported but then not considered urgent – may have been the culprit."

The poor guy next to me suddenly melted to the floor and started flapping around, moaning about his family.

"What's with him?" I asked the waiter.

"His wife and kids were on that vessel," he said polishing some glasses.

Oh Jeez. Well, I was sorry. Truly, genuinely sorry.

"Look," I said, kneeling next to the guy flopping on the ground. "You can't really blame me if my zapper kind of slipped, you know, and fell under my seat while I was packing. I mean, how was I supposed to notice?"

The guy flopped some more, calling out names that wouldn't have tripped so lightly over my tongue.

"Pull yourself together," I said. "What I'm trying to tell you is that the rest of it was the dumbest bad luck: I mean, how many times has it happened to you that you forget to turn something off?"

"What the hell are you talking about?" the waiter said, catching the last part of the conversation. "That guy's about to croak and you're apologizing to him for not turning something off."

"You're right," I said, returning to my stool and ordering another drink. "You're absolutely right. I should mind my own bloody business."

So I did and they came and took the guy away and the rest of it you know.

# RULES OF CONDUCT

**I.**
What a lovely number.
Who am the number I?

**II.**
My name, as I said before, is Givens. My nocturnal life belongs to me, you understand. Mine and mine alone. And it's totally unregulated. There's not much to do at night, however, but to curl up and sleep. Darkness isn't *like* a blanket – it *is* a blanket. The city is shut down, streets and all; the trees and the stars are locked away, deposited within the safety of computer memory banks. No principle is involved here, only the standard rules. In the morning, I'm handed a cube by the man who waits at my door. Snevig, of course, is his name.

A Givens has always had a Snevig waiting at his door with a bright, sun-catching cube in his hand. One can't possibly exist without the other. I don't have to accept the cube Snevig hands me. No, nothing says I do. I may throw it back in his face or smash it into millions of crystal smithereens – which reunite within seconds. In fact, I did just that once, saying I needed no cube guidelines for my life. Snevig simply pulled out another cube from his chest cavity and held it out. But I slammed the door in his face before he could hand it to me.

For those who haven't imagined it, the feeling is unimaginable. I was free, free to do as I pleased, free to go where I wanted when I wanted. But, then, after the initial act of rebellion, the initial gush of emotion, I realized this vast emptiness before me, this chasm of there-was-nothing-I-could-do because I'd lost the directions, I'd destroyed the instructions. One step at a time, I told myself. Go back to the basics. That might help. I tried opening the front door. My hand couldn't grasp the handle. Think quickly! Think of the rules from previous days. There must be some out there that can help you. But none came to mind or, if they did, they were totally inappropriate for the present situation.

For example, I suddenly remembered the rules for digging a grave, for building a rocket ship, for diverting a river. I stood there, muscles binding, unable even to work out how I'd moved my legs. Or turned my head. Out of the corner of my eye, I could see through the window; I could see all the people walking about purposefully, cube in hand, full of determination and vigour. How I envied their vigour, their sense of knowing what they were doing – and how to do it.

The day passed this way. I grew hungry and thirsty. But not even my stomach remembered how to rumble properly. My thoughts, which were more and more like a scrambled stream of consciousness, could hardly be described as thoughts, but rather simply the random firing of nerve patterns. I was bathed in perspiration, longing for the following morning, the knock on the door that would set me in motion again.

You can imagine with what joy I accepted my rules, held the cube to my chest, then rushed to slip it into the decoding machine. I thought I detected a smile on Snevig's face, but that's impossible. He has no smiling apparatus. Later that morning, while raking a selection of perfect leaves (gorgeous, aren't they?), I found in their midst the reassembled cube I'd rejected the previous day. The First Rule said: "Please reject the rules given you today." The infantile thoughts I'd had of rebellion vanished like a child's whim, like the pathetic dream wishes of an idiot.

## III.

The Givenses and the Snevigs have no doubt changed drastically down through the years, though what those changes could be I can't imagine. Their changes, however, have always been as a unit. And always Snevig has handed out the rules while Givens has accepted them. Snevig doesn't make the rules, mind you. Someone else – a Nevig or Levig or Sevig – draws them up. Still others process them through the cubes. At this point, the links become fuzzy and disconnected. Many take the drawer-upper for the maker, but that's simply not true. He's more like the court scribe with an electronic cube inscriber instead of a quill. Besides, who would accept rules made by someone who so closely resembles you and with whom you have daily commerce?

One can see it's only a myth, a misguided attempt to put a human face on something that is strictly of a bureaucratic nature. Computers are needed to handle, sort out, store and distribute the countless cubes containing what are officially – and somewhat literally – known as Rules of Conduct. Out of habit, we speak of the computers as "making" these rules. By this is meant only the physical act of producing the cubes and inscribing them with the rules. These rules retain a general, overall configuration but each is tailored for a particular and specific person. There is no hint of chance involved. Each has the stamp of individuality on it. Mine is GI (22-5-14-19), a unique conjunction that serves to define me not only to others but to myself as well.

Why am I telling you this? The Fourth Rule in this morning's cube suggested I "attempt a literate, but not esoteric, rendition of our social lives as an example of metonymy for the new group of archives soon to be created." A new way to keep me busy, to give me purpose. Archives are always being created to provide coverage and verisimilitude for an expanding world. In them are kept the duplicates of every Rule of Conduct ever handed out. It is considered a signal honour to open one. Not the greatest honour – that is reserved for the closing of an archive – but of great conversational value and necessary for advancement of any sort.

Nivens, my next-door neighbour, is horribly jealous of me (his Second Rule for the day) and waits anxiously for the opportunity to put the official seal on an archive, even his own. We snub each other on the street. I'm comforted by the feeling we would do so even if not so ordered.


IV.

The Rules of Conduct are divided between the trivial and the meaningful. This is deceiving terminology for one not used to our semantics since the titles have little to do with the content and it doesn't pay to put too much meaning into them. This morning's cube, for example, contains under the trivial heading Rule One: "Do not shake hands with anyone" and Rule Three:

"Your eyesight will continue to worsen now that it's summer. Blindness will be the end product." Under the meaningful were Rule Two: "Proceed to Simulated Centre Cemetery and place flowers on hologram of your mother's grave" and the already mentioned Fourth Rule.

One of yesterday's rules was a suggestion that I discover the pattern behind the use of the terms "trivial" and "meaningful." I failed in the sense that I could not find a common quality of triviality or meaningfulness except by labelling them all trivial or meaningful. Or labelling them at random. But that's ridiculous for Rules of Conduct, in the formal manner here used, are absolutely necessary to life. In fact, they might be called Rules of Life if it weren't for the slightly pedantic taste this leaves in one's mouth.

What would happen if all of us suddenly decided to disregard these rules? I remembered vividly the day I rejected my cube. What would occur if Snevig decided he no longer would hand me my cube? Would we all freeze, unable to move? Or worse, would we go out into the streets, stumbling blindly, wandering aimlessly, bumping into one another and inanimate objects, driving nowhere, growing old in garbage cans?

Rumours circulate of pre-rule days when these were the conditions universally accepted. Horrendous novels describe these meanderings endlessly, page after boring page. One of the best was called *The Free-Will Syndrome* in which the characters were presented a choice between such standard themes as heroism and cowardice, the virgin and the whore, coitus inversus and a tergo, ascot and tie. Another was *Apathetic Sympathy: The Story of a Metaphysical Rebel*, written by the officer who executed said rebel. They are silly frivolous things in the manner of all pre-rule writing, left now purely for our amusement

24

(when the rules so dictate). Intellectually, we need nothing but the rules. They are both philosophy and art, both religion and fiction, both meaning and demeaning.


## V.

Snevig is teaching me how to read in Braille for I'll be blind soon. When I first discovered that my eyes were deteriorating and that – although there existed specialists who could cure me – I wouldn't be able to make contact with them, I acted in a childish manner (Rule Two for that day). I panicked, attempted to return the rules to Snevig, thus pretending I'd never seen them. I pleaded with him to give me another set – just for once. Nivens', for example. But I was simply throwing a tantrum. I knew what I asked was impossible. Rules of Conduct are inexorable and deny all pretence. I had only to look at the expression on Snevig's face to realize that.

The funny thing, however, is that I haven't noticed the least change in my eyesight. Perhaps that is due to the relative perspective involved, a change in the structure of the cubes themselves to compensate. More tactility, perhaps. Or increased audio participation. At any rate, blindness will come in one stroke, although I shall have gone through all the steps of semiblindness and visual deterioration. When blind, I can, thanks to Snevig, continue to follow the rules.

He informs me that these rules, in keeping with the new "feel" bumps and knobs on the cubes, will become more physical as time goes by. Mountain climbing courses, he assures me, will be the norm and I can look forward to at last getting my driver's licence (denied me thus far for poor eye-hand coordination). He also says that the central computer, once it discovers your particular defect, indulges in all sorts of practical jokes. It may, for example, order you to read the entire library of Middle English Literature in the original or to enrol in the School for Retired Firepersons.

I'm anticipating an old age replete with adventure and good fortune. Sivens, the neighbour on my left who is ordered daily to suffer from amnesia, wanted to shake hands with me earlier in the day. I declined, giving my hurry to get to the cemetery as an excuse for not stopping to chat. Sivens is naturally prone to talk for hours and even bothers strangers to have a word with them, to ask questions such as: "What are those things waving like trees in the wind?" Trees, you say. Ah, he says. Those things waving like trees in the wind are trees.

Tragic, yes, but one can't help the rules one is given. It would be like questioning one's existence. Or separating oneself into essence and existence. No, I wasn't in any hurry to see such a dubious person as my mother. My mother? What a queer way of expressing a purely symbolic gesture for a purely symbolic creature. Not even the rules can erase totally the old-fashioned terms that acted out their own demented rules.

Why, there was a time when mothers were actually living beings and not simulated holograms resting in peace forever, when the word itself carried with it enough instruction and protocol to last a lifetime. Nothing wrong with that. The problem was that such words were vague, ill-defined and, worst of all, gave the impression there was a choice in the matter, that one could do otherwise, for example, than honour thy mother. Impressions of this type led to the rash of mother killings near the chaotic end of the pre-rule days.

## VI.

You may well ask what the point of this is. It has been asked (in one of the strangest rules I've ever come across). Why indulge in the game of existence when all the moves are made for you, now and forever? Why pretend a struggle of decisions and choices when only a blank memory remains to back up these words? There are many reasons, of which I have been ordered to know but a few: to remove all fear of nihilism and anarchy, carelessness or intentional mischief; to create beautiful patterns of order and disorder; to know you can step out safely onto the street without being sucked up through space toward the searing eye of the sun.

If one of the rules orders A to rob a bank, another will command B to arrest him. C will have instructions to judge; D injects the drug that permits A to return to society. And so on, in a delicate and complex building of action, reaction and interaction. Motives and sublimations never come into play, unless it is so ruled. If either A or B is shot in the process of carrying out their rules, it won't cause a general panic. Wars are conducted in a series of negotiated advances and retreats between our computer and the enemy's, with only an increase in the spewing out of cubes to indicate what is happening. Simple and neat. The cleanliness of order within seeming disorder.

The disturbing factor in all this is death, naturally: it is the only thing not regulated. Yet. Some, however, believe that the time of your death is also known in advance (from where, no one is sure), but you're not told for fear that the shock might cause irreparable damage to your rule-control centre. Very commendable, if true. Still, death continues to appear to be a natural event that has remained entirely so, unintelligent and chaotic. Or so we are led to believe. By? By the same ones, I guess, who are preparing us for our great mission in life. Not us, individually, of course. Us as a species.

Another puzzling aspect of our lives on which this idea of some future purpose might shed light is the uncommon but regular occurrence of the Circular Rule. As an example, take Rule X: "Please disobey all rules on this cube." This particular rule has baffled the minds of generations of social philosophers, i.e. those concerned with the genesis of rules, commands and instructions. There are sad cases of individuals who receive this rule on the first day of adulthood (the earliest date of which we have any memory) and they spend the rest of their lives analyzing it, working it out and failing to accomplish anything. They haunt the streets with a blank look on their faces.

For every tortured step forward they advance, you can rest assured they will take one back. The problem lies in the fact that, if one disobeys all rules as ordered, it follows that Rule X must also be disobeyed. Therefore, all rules are to be obeyed, which once again leads back to the original Rule X, also to be obeyed. The solution to this will probably lead to the solution of an entire pyramid of unanswerables, perhaps even that curious disintegration called death. Coding "Please disobey all rules but this one" is simply giving a new rule and also evading the issue. This is the cycle of language that even our Rules of Conduct haven't been able to break.

Or were they meant to break it in the first place?


## VII.

Rule Five, under the meaningful heading: "You are to blame Snevig for your approaching blindness because he did nothing to prevent it, to get you to see a specialist on time. Instead, he accepted the situation with a look of pity and a shrug." Snevig caused my blindness! Of course! How could I have been so stupid not to realize that?

Rule Six, under the trivial heading: "Before the setting of the sun, a glorious sight in the lull between coming and going, you will invite Snevig to dinner (pre-packaged macaroni and cheese casserole plate). You will hesitate before putting on the second layer of macaroni and sprinkle poison (your choice) between it and the first. This is for heinous crimes against your body – and therefore the species. He will be replaced immediately."

Poor Snevig. Does he know? Parts of it perhaps. Shall I use arsenic trioxide? I know nothing about poisons. Strychnine? The decision seems to have been left up to me. Snevig qualifies as my one friend, my one true companion. He has taught me how to react calmly at the thought of impending blindness and has given me invaluable assistance on what to do when I actually can no longer see. I can now "read" Braille with incredible speed, knowing instinctively which side of the cube to touch, to press.

It's senseless to poison him, absurd in the most destructive way. Without his guidance, I'll be lost, and who knows if I'll ever adjust to the new Snevig. What if he's talkative and laughs all the time? Or else wishes to play cards? Enjoys running his hand through his hair? Or mine? Pretends to know all the answers? I couldn't take someone like that. It would drive me mad. And Snevig, poor Snevig. An elegy for Snevig: He served me well as far as we could tell – and the rules allowed. Rule Seven as a postscript on the flip side: "The body of the traitor (previously known as Snevig) will be removed by means of the portable crematorium. It will make the rounds of the neighbourhood and arrive at your house early tomorrow morning. Please leave the body on the curb."

## VIII.

Snevig died last night with some type of fixed smile on his face. A piece of macaroni dribbled from his cheek. He flushed it down with wine, looked at me (a cleansing?) and slumped in his chair. I checked through his rules and found they were the complements of mine except that the poisoning wasn't mentioned. Did he read mine? Had he been reading them all along? Was he simply the messenger who brought a bottle of unknown substance to me as a gift ("What are friends for, after all?")?

I'll not die that way. I'll fight. If it's in the rules. I didn't sleep at all. Rather, I kept vigil over the body. The night, I discovered, is the time for the recovering of individual purpose and feeling. This was very unnerving. Why isn't the night also ordered by a series of rules? Black, slimy, carbon-copy cubes that suck in, absorb all light? Everything tells me that, logically, it probably is, that its formlessness is simply a system of random but conforming particles. Or is it left alone on purpose so that creatures like me, who carry their satchels of doubt like bile, may have an outlet for all the thoughts and actions not yet regulated, arising from the primeval slime?

A thought came to me. What if, let's say, I felt guilty for something I'd done? Let's say, because of this, I decided to form a plan by which I could destroy the whole cube-handers echelon, drawer-uppers, computers, and makers. Let's say this plan was beautifully conceived, simple, well-timed and utterly obvious – straight from a pre-rule novel. It was a great plan, I found myself thinking at the time. But it has one flaw – I've forgotten it. Something vague remains about its essence being a series of link-cutting steps, a destruction of the messenger system so no cubes could be handed out. No one would've attempted to stop me since rules don't apply at night. Or do they?

## IX.

Two new men at my door this morning. One small and unsmiling; the other large and capable of minor affability. No names attached. They handed me the cube in unison, stuffed Snevig's body head first into the portable crematorium and then departed. I watched them go down the street, a puff of smoke rising lazily from their machine. Under the combined heading of trivial and meaningful, the only Rule for the day:

"Congratulations. You have passed all your tests successfully. Now, we wish to inform you that your blindness was invented by us to shake you out of a spreading lethargy in which your thoughts dwelt too much on what you were encoding. This form of lethargy is becoming prevalent in our society. Granted, much of the fault lies with us, but it must be curbed. As a consequence and from a fear of your perceived blindness, you took the life, through poisoning, of one Snevig, known as your symbiotic twin – SN (5-22-9-7). A commendable act and very much in accordance with the rules.

"As a reward for services rendered, it is my duty – and pleasure – to inform you that, as of today, no further rules will be given to you. Think of it as an experiment – an experiment with no chance of success, of course – toward a future dissolution. No hard feelings, eh? P.S.: If you wish, you may scream."


## X.

'X' marks the spot. The numbers have changed. When am I? What are those trees waving in the wind like trees?

# ISHOP BERKELEY AMONG THE MATERIAL SAVAGES

NARRATOR:

In 1728, George Berkeley, the pre-eminent British philosopher, sets sail for the New World in the hopes of "establishing a college in Bermuda for American Indians." It is his belief, his dream, that, by doing so, he can help spread both British culture and religion. But the closest Berkeley gets to Bermuda is Newport, Rhode Island, and the man who maintained that "to be is to be perceived" returns home deeply disappointed in 1732. It is on this long and arduous trip that Berkeley, sick, delirious, and confined for several months below deck, has an extraordinary [dare one say, hallucinatory] vision. A vision within a vision.

❦

## WHAT HE SEES

A gigantic clock hovering overhead with only two settings: Zeno-zero and the most split of seconds. Both hands on Zeno-zero.

Neither hand has ever been seen to move. Written below the clock face: "The first argument asserts the non-existence of motion on the ground that that which is in locomotion must arrive at the half-way stage before it arrives at the goal." Clock overlooks what is affectionately called the University Club. The Club is created by its members as they need it. Members appear and disappear on cue, being little more than random collections of sub-atomic particles floating in electromagnetic fields.

NARRATOR:
When Berkeley first hears rumours of material savages on the other side of the as-yet-nonexistent galactic wheel, he pretends not to show too much interest. In fact, he barely raises an eyebrow to acknowledge the words – savages, other side, galactic wheel – buzzing around him.

BERKELEY:
(*sitting in an overstuffed chair and to himself*) Let the others do the spadework. I'm not going to be backed into an indefensible position again.

NARRATOR:
But, as everyone knows, that is more easily said than done. The other members at the University Club are well aware of Berkeley's ideas on the subject and the fact he'd been blistered by a barrage of criticism [not to mention mockery] for just such speculation in his thesis.

VOICE:
Well, young Berkeley, what say you?

NARRATOR:
Berkeley looks up in the direction of the voice, at the same time recreating the portion of the room he needs.

BERKELEY:
(*again to himself*) Gad, it's that insufferable equalitarian Locke, a toe-the-line bower and scraper whose one claim to fame is having once unwittingly encouraged a revolution in a tea pot colony. A tea pot colony that had been his making in the first place. Freedom and liberty for all, indeed.

NARRATOR:
By the glint in his eye, Berkeley knows the pale anemic blob floating before him is out for a bit of high-minded blood.

BERKELEY:
(*holding out and looking at the back of a well-manicured hand*) What say I to what?

LOCKE:
(*easing himself onto the chandelier*) Come, come, young Berkeley. There's no need to be coy. We're all aware of your predeliction for and interest in that oxymoronic species known commonly and fondly as material savages. As I recall, it was the basis for a passionate if not well thought-out paper, was it not? A sadly impoverished attempt to disprove: "No man's knowledge can go beyond his experience."

BERKELEY:
Old Locke, don't you think it's a bit impolitic to bring up a young man's well-meaning confusions? After all, a quick glance at any of our complete editions and...

NARRATOR:
There is a collective groan from the rest of the room as one by one the others pop into view. Descartes tears off a huge chunk of fingernail and spits it into the fireplace; Hume cracks two billiard balls together, seemingly interested in the space between them; Leibniz makes a pretense of examining a point several metres in front of him; Zeno of Alea lifts one leg and freezes; and Aquinas, de facto spiritual father of the Club and much easier to take since dropping his claim to sainthood, snorts before falling back into a substantial sleep.

LOCKE:
(*smiling nervously, using facial muscles seldom exercised*) You're absolutely right. I tried to take unfair advantage. Do forgive me.

BERKELEY:
(*waving a kerchief before replacing it in his sleeve*) Consider it done, old man. We all make mistakes.

LOCKE:
In a manner of speaking...

DESCARTES:
There are many manners of speaking...

LEIBNIZ:
Speaking in a mannerly way…

NARRATOR:
And they're off on a discussion of the semantic implications of the phrase: And the word was made flesh. On any other occasion, Berkeley would be right in the middle of it, blasting with every ounce of the prodigious brain power in his possession. For what else has the University Club to do but discuss, argue, tear thoughts apart and reconstruct them forever and a day? This time, however, he sinks back into his plush velvet chair and dreams of a different future.

BERKELEY:
(*to himself*) It's an incredibly risky one. Perhaps one that doesn't even exist. Or that leads to madness, a sad peculiar condition that leaves one trapped in circularity and infinite regression. Witness the New Pyrrhonian skeptics who manage to undo all claims to knowledge before wishing themselves into nonexistence.

NARRATOR:
But he has to try, if only to test the courage of his convictions. For as long as he can remember, he has been George Berkeley, University Club member, Fellow of the Closed Order of Immaterials [the only provable, registered inhabitants of the universe], and Eternal Guardian of the Word. He, along with a dozen or so other [non]entities, are all that's left of an experiment long gone awry, an experiment none of them knows anything about, having come *a priori*. And he realizes full well that rumours of material savages are most likely simply that – or else

one of those impractical jokes that Wittgenstein and Quine are infamous for. Gavigai, indeed!

❦

But that doesn't keep him from his preparations. For anyone who's read his abandoned thesis, *On Materiality: Speculation That Independent Life Forms Exist*, with the least bit of care, these preparations would be self-explanatory. First he put together what he calls his t-span solar sailer [the *S.S. Hylas*], a billowing criss-crossed contraption much like a spiderweb, except that it's made literally of infinitesimally small strands of shining immaterial. It's this that will fly him to the other end of the galaxy. Or so he hopes. Actually it doesn't really fly at all. It's a matter displacer. In other words, instead of bringing him to the coordinates indicated, it brings the coordinates to him. At least, that's the theory. Oh yes, he knows all about his colleague Descartes' well-founded objections – how time and space can't logically exist, how all things are instantiated in one place and that place has form but no matter and all that – but he doesn't care. There are some things one must take on faith – and damned be explanations and objections. The proof, after all, is in the doing. With him he brings [and these are all explained in the thesis] detectors, transplanters, converters and de-materializers.

Of course, he keeps all this from his fellow Immaterialists [or Realists as some prefer to call themselves]. Aside from the fact that old idiot Locke would heap scorn on him, their arguments can be quite persuasive – as has to be the case if they really believe it's this thinking that holds together the fabric of the mental universe – and he might easily be convinced to drop the whole scheme. So he prefers to say nothing of material savages and keep up as much as possible the pretense that there's little more to life than their daily round of discussions in the University Club. To his credit, no one suspects a thing [except perhaps Aquinas who has a nose for even the tiniest alteration in an argument's sequence – have you ever tried to argue sloppily with God?] right up to the day he appears in the Club's plushly carpeted foyer wrapped like a cocoon in the S.S. *Hylas*.

❧

LOCKE:
(*cadaver head under his arm*) I simply must have the name of your tailor. That outfit is divine.

BERKELEY:
I've come to say goodbye.

NARRATOR:
Several of the members gasp; others begin to expound all at once, babbling in unison about the impossibility of goodbyes in a world where the inhabitants are always together. By definition.

BERKELEY:
Apparently, some aren't.

LOCKE:
(*fountain of blood gushing from his severed carotid artery*) And you're off to seek them out?

BERKELEY:
That's right.

NARRATOR:
There's a general uproar. His good friend Descartes rushes toward him, thinking perhaps to physically restrain him or some such impossibility; Leibniz produces one of his tiresome black boxes, a sure sign he's disturbed; Zeno of Alea [not to be mistaken for the Citium Zeno who rarely says or does anything] tries to shake his head; and Aquinas mutters something about substance and makes a motion with his hands that could be either a blessing or a curse. Only Locke, head replaced and bouncing along the ceiling, laughing so hard his entire body quivers, seems to be having a good time.

LOCKE:
(*snorting and guffawing*) Oh my. I haven't been so royally entertained since Russell flew up his own nether eye claiming he'd found the flaw in Gödel's Incompleteness Theorem. Bravo! Bravo!

BERKELEY:
Goodbye. Wish me luck.

NARRATOR:
He starts shaking the web about him and, surrounded by an almost visible humming, vanishes from their sight. His only regret is that he can't see the look on Locke's face at the moment he proves despite all logic there indeed is an elsewhere.

# WHERE IS HE?

But an elsewhere nothing like he could have imagined [which, of course, would have defeated the whole enterprise]. At first, he allows himself the freedom of travelling through the medium undetermined. All about him, the cities of the material savages whirl like whimsical wind-blown creations. They don't seem real but he knows this is an illusion, a result of his not yet having activated the detection machinery. Thus he is able to float through solid barriers and listen to the hum of their molecular activity [just like his thesis had predicted], the furry balls of energy trying desperately to stay bundled together, to struggle against their inevitable defeat. Ah, Berkeley thinks, so this is entropy. Well, well. I wonder what Zeno [of Elea] would say.

Entropy? Bah! "All motion is an illusion." Before one deteriorates to nothing, one would have to deteriorate half-way. And so on and so forth. Ergo, either we are impossible or it is. I leave the choice to you. All so simple, eh Zeno?

Berkeley switches on the detectors. Suddenly, it feels as if there is no more room for both him and the molecules. With a quantum pop, he finds himself out in the open, floating above a ribbon of black dotted with white stripes. The solar sailer bounces off one of the massive canyon walls between edifices and rises toward the sunlight, eager for the anti-photon wind that drives it. As he flies by, Berkeley can reach out and pass his fingers along the nearest structure. The rough, chipped substance leaves no doubt about its materiality. This is so real it hurts. Skin scrapes away. Raw red marks appear on his fingers. There is even a fine trickle of blood along the inside of his palm. But that isn't the best of it. Berkeley feels a sharp pang of delight as he takes in the warmth of the sun, feels the wave/particles deflecting against the sailer. There are shadows in the air, murky and undefined at the moment. But their significance leaves Berkeley reeling with anticipation. No matter what the risk, he knows he can't stop at this first level of contact, which could be described as proximate one-way at best. He wants the entire run of experience, one which means a multi-sided interaction and all the dangers therein inherent. For there is sentient life here. Or an analog so close as to be indistinguishable. [What need you proof of existence when you have essence? Aquinas would ask. Of what use is essence when you can't prove you exist? Descartes would retort. I've found both! Berkeley wants to shout.]

He takes a deep breath and flips the transplanter. If it works as self-advertised… Oh my… There follows a dizziness, a queasy slimy feeling. For the first time since achieving consciousness, Berkeley is psychically blind. He doesn't know who he is. Or where. He feels heat and a blast of stench. Something is probing him, penetrating and then pulling out again with a rhythmic pendulum motion. Other instruments tug at him, grip him, squeeze him for a moment before releasing. He senses a frenzy, a mounting tension. Semi-words sputter, break upon him. Harsh words, meaningless yet bitter. The probe increases, rises to fever pitch and then explodes. Like a thick gusher inside him. Flooding him with warmth and the thought of invasion. He begins to see. Tiny swimmers in a sticky soup. The battle for possession.

"Bitch!" a harsh voice bellows.

The jolt hurtles him across space, almost knocks him senseless.

"You fucking cold bitch! I'll teach you. You're all mine now – to do with as I please."

And once again the probe, this time from a different direction, blind-sided, flesh being torn away, shredded, ripped with brutal delight.

"I've been watching you on the other side – all smug and sweet innocence. You've had this coming for a long time."

Berkeley feels the darkness surround him again as lights dim and the cruel voices fade. He senses something beyond his comprehension, a change or passage of some kind. For what had been there before, what he had felt so strongly, no longer exists. [What exists cannot pass into non-existence, Leibniz would counter mildly.] All that remains is an immeasurably cold void. This must be death, Berkeley says, just before the darkness takes him.

When he awakes, the first thing that strikes him is the stench: vomit, blood, semen, urine, all tossed together in an unholy salad with him lying right in the middle of it. His tongue clings thickly to his mouth; the back of his head pulses with pain; there is a wetness between his legs, a clammy glue that dribbles weakly away. He opens his eyes. Enormous blank walls stare down at him from all sides. In the distance the faint glow that indicates dawn. He struggles to stand up and manages it only by leaning against the nearest wall. Never before has he felt such pain, such an intrusion on his ability to reason. Oh, he's often experimented with what he thought of as physical pain, or rather with what he thought pain would be like if he'd had a body. A real body. But it wasn't like this, not the remotest like this. Merely blinking causes his head to throb; muscles spasm in their reprieve from rigor mortis; his abdomen contracts, and he manages to squat just in time before unleashing a bloody diarrheal flood that leaves his rectum burning and itching so badly he wants to reach in and yank his intestines out.

Just when Berkeley thinks he can take no more, it starts to rain. A warm, flower-scented rain. Slowly at first, pinging against his flesh and bursting into tiny suds. He rubs himself, feels the cleansing, healing substance close his wounds and wash away the grime. Then it falls harder, gathering in rivulets to dissolve the stench on the street and carry it away through well-concealed gratings. Perhaps, life as a material savage isn't so bad after all, he says to himself, arching back so the rain can run down his front, can spill down his chest, can relieve the ache, the sense of violation that still clings to him. After a few moments, the rain halts. A drying wind, thick with the odour of pollen, fluffs up his shoulder-length hair. The sun appears between buildings, casting its reddish light against perfectly reflective material. For the first time, he can see himself. And as he looks at his reflection, he begins to laugh. This is something that had never occurred to him. Nor to any of the theorists of the University Club. But of course the whole thing is a coin toss, 50-50 right down the middle as the Probabilists liked to say. Has he won or lost the toss? The handsome mammaries topped by stiff brown nipples; soft, billowy buttocks; the thick clutch of hair between his legs; the swell of the vaginal mound. Here is a fine specimen of the female species, a wonderful reproductive machine. Win some, lose some, he decides. He stretches languorously, soaking in the pleasant sun, then starts to walk through the identical grid-like avenues on the sides of which buildings shoot up straight to the sky as if organic, as if they hadn't been built but rather grew there through some alchemy of their own.

Quite advanced for material savages, Berkeley thinks. I wouldn't have put them at this stage. Speaking of which, where are they? Aside from the attack – that it had been an attack of some sort he has no doubt – and the harsh voices, he has seen no others. Nor has he heard a single sound. Curious for a city this size, a place that seemed to stretch endlessly in every direction. Where are the occupants of these buildings, the workers that made this material reality function, the vehicles, the traffic, the construction, the beasts and machines of burden? He walks on, not sure if he is actually getting anywhere or simply going in elaborate circles. But no, the sun is moving in the sky above him and, by following it, he can tell whether or not he is advancing. Finally, with the sun almost directly overhead, he comes to a break in the structures, a massive square perhaps a kilometre by a kilometre whose base seems to be made of the same materials as the buildings, except that it is smoky and translucent in places, almost like a river frozen in glass. Roads, identical to the one he is on, empty into it from all sides. It glitters and sparkles in the sunlight and feels warm beneath his feet. Berkeley lies down on it, pressing his body flat against it so that every possible centimetre of him is touching, is making contact. It pulses. Like a creature gone into hibernation. Just enough to send friendly shivers through his body and raise a glow that radiates from the base of his skull, around the aureoles of his nipples, in the heat of his loins. Berkeley has shaken the hair out of his eyes and is turning to make contact with his other cheek when he sees it – another creature, fur-covered, crouched and moving furtively along the far edge of the square, perhaps 100 metres away.

"I say!" he shouts, in his soprano voice, standing up and waving.

The other creature freezes.

"I say. Hello there."

As Berkeley heads toward it, the other creature, whom he now recognizes as an older female clad in some kind of mangy fur that covers her reproductive organs but not her sagging breasts, lets out a scream and breaks into a limping run – in the opposite direction.

"Wait!" Berkeley shouts. "I won't hurt you. I just wish to talk. Wait!"

The creature stops for a moment, turns toward him rubbing her eyes as if in disbelief and then flees again. Berkeley takes off after her, knowing he'll quickly lose her in the maze-like streets if he doesn't keep her in sight. But, with her limp, it isn't long before he catches up to her.

"Hold on, I say. I won't hurt—"

A knife gleams from within the fur and slashes forward. Berkeley jumps back just in time. The creature, her face a mask of absolute terror, growls a low warning, a hiss like a feral cat with its back up. She then begins to limp away again. Berkeley follows a safe distance behind and they enter once again the streets surrounded by giant skyscrapers, this time with the sun sloping in front of them. Several times, Berkeley tries talking to the creature but is completely ignored. Almost as if he weren't there. Or at least as if the creature has made up her mind he really isn't there. He is on the verge of approaching her again, of trying one more time to communicate, when they burst from the streets, from the buildings, into a low encampment under a molten sky that seems to drip nothing so much as venom. From what he can see, the camp consists of a dozen or so measly tents, shreds really, held together by the most rudimentary stitching. There is dust everywhere and the smell of decay.

The older female stops in the middle of this encampment and lets out a shout, pointing at Berkeley. Others, clad in the same way, appear from within the tents. There are both male and female but they all have the same reaction when they see him: a combination of fear and awe, a shrinking from even the slightest contact.

"April, is that you?" a deep voice says. "No, it can't be."

"It's not April," the female who has led him there says. "April's dead."

"April's dead and gone," the others say all together as if in a practiced litany.

"Then this must be a spirit," the female says. "It followed me here to eat our souls."

"Aghast!" the others cry. "To eat our souls."

"I'm not a spirit," Berkeley says. "And I'm not dead."

"Shoo, shoo," the deep voice says. [Berkeley sees it was coming from one of the larger males.] "Go back into the city."

"Go, go," the others sing/plead/order. "Go to devour or be devoured."

"And what if I decide to stay?"

Everyone gasps and they cover their eyes.

"You can't stay!" the female says. "There is no place for you here. Our souls are safe. Your spells don't work."

"No souls, no souls," they chant.

"See here. I'm staying," Berkeley says, squatting down cross-legged and pretending to examine his pubic hair. "What are you going to do about it?"

"We'll kill you," the deep-voiced one says.

"Kill you, kill you," the others repeat.

Berkeley shrugs.

"Kill her," the deep-voiced one commands the older female.

She rushes forward, knife held over her head. And stops abruptly a few metres away. Berkeley looks up and shakes his hair in a gesture of contempt. Just as he's thought. He laughs. It is a sweet feminine laugh.

"Truly it sounds like April, my playmate," one of the younger females says. "Could it be…"

"No, no!" the others scream. "It isn't possible. April is dead. She spent the night in the city. There's no escape."

"I escaped," Berkeley says.

"You are not April," the deep-voiced one says.

"Not April," the others repeat.

"You're a spirit wrapped in April's body," the older female says. "I saw you sucking away her soul."

"Not April, not April."

"Let's retire to consult, shall we?" the deep-voiced one says.

"Yes," the others answer. "Consultation is a must."

They move away, shuffling through the dust. One of them squats and releases a stream of water. Now this is more like it, Berkeley thinks. This is my idea of material savages. Except it really isn't. For he can't understand the juxtaposition of the city and the encampment; the marble-like floor and the dirt; the gleaming buildings and the shabby tents. As well, the very air itself is different here: turbulent, unclear, constantly changing. More… more natural. That's it, of course. But the naturalness is completely undermined by the ordered forest of buildings [if that's what they were for he'd seen no entrances, no place from which to view the outside world] and the empty streets. There is, he sees looking up, no slow progression from one to the other. The marble-like material and the structures fall off abruptly to become this humble camp of tents. Yet, at the same time, no dirt encroaches on the city.

He stands up and stretches. The savages, having consulted, are scuffling back toward him, walking in a tight group that looks all the more pathetic against the background of heavy, violet-coloured clouds and swirling dust. They stop some 20 metres away. Several scruffy children are peering fearfully from behind their parents' legs.

"Oh, April-like creature," the adults say as one, "we have consulted and come to a decision."

"Good," Berkeley says as nonchalantly as possible. "I was getting a bit hungry."

The deep-voiced one and the older female step forward, holding hands: "We have decided that, since it isn't possible for you to be alive, we must consider you as not-there."

And they all turn and go about their business.

"What do you mean, not-there?" Berkeley says, laughing to conceal his growing irritation. "How can I be not-there when I'm standing right before you? Look. This is flesh and blood. Like yours. You bloody fools! You bunch of cretins! You... you..."

But how long can one keep up insults when no one's paying attention, when even the dogs pretend to be busy with other things? Besides, he says to himself, they're right. I'm not April. April's dead. I felt her death myself. And I am a spirit. Of sorts. Although that's academic, isn't it? At this moment, I'm nothing but George Berkeley inside this female savage's body and I'd better make the most of it. Meaning what? Live and learn, learn and live, like any material creature must do.

Berkeley walks proudly to the centre of the encampment where a wizened old man is sitting, pounding red grain in a bowl. ·

"Hello," he says, squatting beside him. "What are you doing there?"

The old man keeps pounding grain, occasionally adding spit to make it more cohesive.

"Can I help you?"

The old man looks up at the sky – brilliant crimson lightning flashing between one cloud and the next – and starts singing softly to himself.

"I guess not, eh? Tell me then: What is the meaning of meaning? Are reality and appearance on a collision course? Is mathematics the foundation of existence?"

Still, no answer. Berkeley spends a few moments examining the long detailed lines that course down the old man's face, then stands up and moves on to a group of children who seem to be tracing geometric patterns and tapping crooked sticks in the dirt. He recognizes it, after a moment, as a childish three-dimensional model of the city. In the centre of it is a piece of dried fruit. One of the young girls – the one who might have been April's playmate – takes something out of her fur and places it on the model. It is a large black beetle, about the size of an adult thumb, whose body seems to glow as it breathes. The beetle remains still for a moment while the girl stares at it and then it begins to speed along the patterns that are meant to be streets. Whenever it hits a "building," it whirs and spins to orient itself. It keeps this up until it arrives at the central square and starts feasting on the fruit. Berkeley reaches in and picks it up.

"Did you make this?" he asks the girl who'd first taken the beetle out. "Did April, your friend?"

Instead of answering, she pulls out another – an exact duplicate – and replaces it on the model. It, too, whirs and hums until reaching the fruit.

"It's beautiful," Berkeley says, persisting, examining the tiny mechanisms for the wings, the delicate gear system, the ruby-like jewel that makes it glow. "No, I don't think any of you made this. You're not smart enough to make this, now are you? No, I didn't think so."

For a second, he thinks the girl will take the bait but she merely looks past him and starts up the same low humming as the old man. The other children follow her lead, each in turn putting down a beetle and allowing it to make its way to the square where it can feed on the dried fruit.

"Well, it was nice talking to you. You don't mind if I keep this, do you? I didn't think you would. Thank you."

Berkeley walks a little bit, testing out his pariah status, dipping into food bowls, interrupting conversations by laughing or making funny noises, turning cartwheels, peeking into tents where couples huddle together in a combination of sexual excitement and a desire for warmth. No one stops him. They simply carry on as if he weren't there. Then, weighed down by a weariness he's never felt before in his life, he lies flat on his back, the beetle in the palm of his hand. As he falls asleep, the hand opens. The beetle begins to crawl over Berkeley's body, leaving a slightly burning feeling in its wake, as if it were in direct contact with his brain, bypassing the central nervous system. It scuttles up one arm, across the neck and face, down the breasts, back up the other arm, then to his toes. Finally, after travelling along the inside of one thigh, it snuggles up in his pubic hair, several strands wrapped round glistening pincers.

And that's where Berkeley remains, right in the middle of the encampment, snoring gently, legs slightly apart and bent at the knee, hair thrown back like a halo around his head. The material savages – those who have no choice in the matter – are careful to step around or over him as they go about their appointed rounds. Occasionally, one of them sits down cross-legged beside him and stares down at him. For the first time in his life, he dreams. He dreams he is back at the University Club, sitting before the warm fireplace, discussing Plato's Cave. Strangely though, it isn't the same University Club he is used to. And those sitting with him resemble his companions but aren't quite them. In fact, it is all too real to be true. That is it. There is too much corporeality in the dream. He can smell Locke's garlicky breath, the stink of age that hangs on Aquinas like a stiff sticky rag; he can see the waxy, unhealthy glow of Descartes' face, his gnawed-off bleeding fingers; he can feel the threadbare chair, the unnatural warmth. And he is uncomfortable, has to squirm and shift if he stays in one position too long, can't keep his hands still, hears the uneven beating of his heart. None of this is possible: breath, age, skin, chair, hands, heart. None of it exists except for his sufferance and then only in an ideal state. Only as a convenient meeting place. He's been infested, he realizes in the midst of his dream, with materiality, a new way of looking at things – as if they really existed.

He awakes with a start. And in the dark. How quickly and routinely this world spins, without caprice, he says to himself, feeling to see if the beetle is still there. It is.

All around him the acrid smell of smoke, the crackling of fires, the sweet sizzling of meat. And voices, low voices whispering against the dark. He lies unmoving, eyes shut, listening. Soon, he can make out individual words – and those who speak them.

"Something must be done."

"There's no telling what the god will do."

"In its anger, it is unreasoning."

"And full of strange beasts. Let us not forget—"

There is a sudden intake of air, as if they are all inhaling as one, fighting for breath against the memory of something too horrible, too monstrous to contain. So this is the other side of being a material savage, Berkeley thinks: the superstition, the fear of the unknown, the unexplainable. He wants to rise and tell them there is nothing to be afraid of. Everything is explainable. Of course. It has to be. After all, it didn't really exist. But he just lies there, listening to the timid, helpless voices.

"We must do something."

"Perhaps, it will leave on its own."

"Yes, there's always that hope."

"Or that the god will come and get it and leave the rest of us in peace."

"Yes, there's a first time for everything."

"But this is an unusual case. No sacrifice has ever returned – alive. Perhaps this is a message from the god. Perhaps—"

Berkeley grows suddenly tired of the conversation. He lets out an exaggerated yawn, stretches and rubs his crotch. The voices die. He rolls over on his side to look out upon a half-dozen small fires winking feebly in the all-encompassing dark. In the sky, the occasional flash of lightning reveals clouds piled high over each other, roiling and surging forward in the direction of the city. Berkeley stands up and heads toward the fire where the deep-voiced one and the limping older female squat. He kneels down in front of the man.

"You're a tiresome lot," he says in his sweet feminine voice, "not worthy of my friendship. Nevertheless, I take pity on you and offer it."

He reaches down into the man's fur covering and unties it. It falls about his ankles. Berkeley does the same to the older female. No one in the camp moves, prepared as they are to accept whatever fate and the fickle, ineffable god offer. Berkeley throws back his hair and takes the man's penis into his mouth. Within seconds, he feels it engorged with blood, a slight pulse running along one side of it. The man tries his best to pretend nothing is happening, to ignore the not-there creature, a suc-cubus, perhaps, who is performing such private, such intimate acts on him. But it isn't long before his body is twitching of its own accord, before the primeval sexual urgency takes over, before Berkeley's mouth is filling with spurts of warm semen. Berkeley looks up smiling at the exhausted deep-voiced one and then, lowering his face between the limping female's legs, deposits the semen into the vaginal opening.

"No genetic strings attached," he says, rising. "Know that I am April and yet that April is dead. Know that I have taken much more from you than you have given me. Know that the true mysteries have nothing to do with gods – and everything."

He shakes the dust from his body and, glimpsing for the last time those living, breathing proofs of material reality, walks away in the direction of the city.

"It leaves us," the deep-voiced one says flatly. "We're saved."

"It leaves and we're saved," the chorus repeats.

"April is dead," the limping older female says.

"Dead, dead, dead," they echo.

Berkeley comes to the edge of the city and steps onto the cool marble. Above him, the clouds roll back, giving way to a sky bloated with stars, strung with unfamiliar constellations. Of course, he says, this is the other side of the galaxy – whatever that means. Berkeley thinks hard of an impossibly webbed con-traption, of anti-photons and matter displacement. He plucks the beetle from between his legs and puts it down. The beetle pauses for a moment, fluttering its wings, and then scurries off, glowing, lighting the way through the eerie dark. Berkeley fol-lows and, within one right angle, the material savages are gone [they might as well never have existed]. He is once more in the intricate, complex architecture of an empty city, hurrying past buildings with no way to get in or out, along streets no amount of traffic could ever wear down. He crosses again the massive square, feels the surging warmth of something flowing beneath his feet, of engines perhaps or conductors of electricity, runs his tongue along the tantalizing smoky glass, hurries after the winking creature that seems to know the city so well. Finally, the beetle stops. There above it, amid a forest of the tallest structures yet seen, some four or five metres up, floats Berkeley's solar sailer. It gives off a soft, sparkling light, like dew dust or a sprinkling of magic powder. Berkeley reaches up, long, delicate fingers mere wisps amid the massive constructs all around them. He strains, stands on his toes, leaps – gracefully at first but then with more and more desperation. The sailer bobs and weaves above him, playfully mocking him. Berkeley tries scrambling up the nearest wall in the hope of leaping across. There is nothing to hold on to, not the slightest crack or defect. He slides to the ground and begins to cry. They are tears of frustration and self-pity. Frustration? Self-pity? My God, what have I stooped to? Berkeley asks himself. Something of the material savage has crept into my makeup. It was only to be expected. He wipes away the tears, knows suddenly what he has to do. The thought comes clearly to his mind, the ugly putrid disgusting thought. He feels a hatred that burns to his core like hot radium gone critical, a destructive meanness that knows no bounds, that attaches itself to warmth, to weakness and forces it to the surface like pus.

Berkeley shudders, feeling as if he's been soiled, and stands up.

"Let's go," he says to the beetle. "I'm ready."

The beetle leads him back to the square and then vanishes. Berkeley never sees how it happens. One moment it is there, glowing and whirring; the next it is gone. But Berkeley has little time to piece together the mystery for he soon realizes he isn't alone. Coming toward him is a naked young man, sleek, blond and glistening all over with oil. Berkeley feels a slight quiver, the hint of a flush spreading outward from around his breasts. Well, he certainly is strong. And tall. And well built. The young man stops in front of him, arms akimbo, breathing through his flared nostrils. Berkeley smiles and thinks of something appropriate to say.

"Hello, I'm—"

Berkeley never finishes the introductions. A backhanded slap catches him on the side of the face and staggers him. There is blood flowing from his nose.

"Bitch!" the young man says in a voice that seems more animal than human. "You dare return. Though how you escaped the first time remains a mystery."

The young man strikes again, this time with a closed fist, smashing Berkeley's nose. Berkeley goes down, unable to balance himself because of the pain and the tears.

"I'm going to kill you, scum! And it will be a pleasure."

The young man kneels down, forcing Berkeley's legs open with his knee. Berkeley struggles to free himself but it is no use. The young man is too strong and too vicious. He lowers himself brutally on to Berkeley, thick and oily, face twisted into a grin.

"I'm going split you open like a ripe tomato, rip you till you'll beg to be put out of your misery."

Berkeley can smell his breath now, that stale, brimstone spew from the depths of hell itself. The young man slams down upon him. There is a tearing sound and his insides burst with pain, burst like a milkweed pod smashed against a tree. But it is even worse when the young man pulls out again. Now he knows how a fish feels when the barb is jerked out of its mouth. It is as if his entire insides have been speared. He gasps and lets out a scream.

"Shut up, bitch! There's no one to hear you. Don't you know that yet? Only a fool would enter the city at night. Only a fool."

And he continues thrusting, tearing at the open wound, breathing more and more heavily. As the rhythm of his assault increases, the young man seems less and less able to control himself. He slaps at Berkeley, bites him viciously, slobbers over him. Then, applying pressure with his thumbs, he starts squeezing Berkeley's neck.

"Goodbye, bitch. There's no escaping this time."

Berkeley struggles and gasps for air. But each time he breathes, the young man tightens his fingers. Berkeley's body jerks this way and that as oxygen is cut off to his brain; his legs scissor up, his back arches, his sphincter muscles go slack. There is blackness everywhere. And stars splattering against a velvet firmament.

"Jeez. If I would've known how much you liked it…"

And liquid pouring out of a transparent vessel. And the foulest of foul smells. And more blackness. More and more blackness. And then of a sudden nothing.

For April is dead.

Berkeley finds himself back in his solar sailer, floating above the city. Even in the dark he can see clearly [no longer tethered to material limitations]. There is a bruised and battered body in the square below. It must have been beautiful once. And tender-hearted. Another creature walks slowly away from it, walks toward a gleaming wall inside of which still another creature walks toward the one walking toward it. They meet at the edge of the wall and melt together, vanishing within its interior. A rain comes, hissing, sizzling, melting all in its path. The beautiful body breaks up into pieces of flesh, into spiritless globs, into shapeless morsels. And is washed away.

Berkeley sighs and switches on the converters. Time is running backwards. The sailer glides through fuzzy shapes that bounce like fluff, frictionless. There are roars in the distance, cascades of energy, untouching billiard balls [ah, Hume, where are you now?]. The sailer shakes a bit, is buffetted gently by the reversing forces. Time to get back to the real world, Berkeley says, and hits the de-materializer.

<hr />

LOCKE:
(*roaring with laughter and scattering rainbows from his mouth*) Travel plans, young Berkeley? You're not going to get too far with that thing.

AQUINAS:
(*lifting his head from his padded rocking chair*) Tut, tut. That's what happens when one doesn't think through one's arguments.

ZENO OF ELEA:
The danger of taking a forward step without the proper calculations, followed by the realization that such a step is not possible. I have a bad feeling about my friend.

ZENO OF CITIUM:

A bad feeling is a commotion of the mind repugnant to reason, and against nature.


DESCARTES:

Oh dear! The poor fellow's entangled in that awful contraption. We must help him out of it.


NARRATOR:

That's the truth. Poor Berkeley's trapped in his own t-span solar sailer, bound by a net of infinitesimally small strings. Of course, he can free himself in a wink but that would mean admitting his original mistake. So he struggles. And the more he struggles, the more he tangles himself. His fellow Club members laughingly rush to his aid, pulling this way and that. And getting themselves caught in the process. In the end, even Locke comes down from the ceiling to lend a hand and soon the entire Club is wrapped in a fine net of laughter and bonhomie. Unheard amid the philosophic rumpus, the clock's forward tick – and one of the hands on the most split of seconds.

⟞⟐⟝

And that might explain why the S.S. *Hylas* now hovers above the familiar canyon wall city [familiar to Berkeley in any case], obsidian structures absorbing all sunlight, while its passengers hang literally by a thread [or perhaps better described as a string]. Below, hungry and rapacious, sleek and oiled, the material savages eagerly await the inevitable falling to earth [despite the presence of good old Zeno] of the last of the Immaterials.

# PARADISE ISLAND[1]
## (ANNOTATED VERSION)

From: Capt. James Cook, on board *H.M.S. Endeavour*
To: His Majesty's Privy Secretary
Date: May 10, 1769

After several weeks of vain searching, it is my sad duty to announce that Paradise Island has vanished into thin air. It has been swallowed up in a sea we have criss-crossed at least a dozen times, have plumbed and scanned with the most powerful instruments aboard. To no avail. Our helmsman has worked the convergence upon that particular point from every possible angle, mapped it beyond any thought of error. No use. The calculations showed us where it had to be, where it must be without fail. But it is not. Only a small turbulence on the surface of the water, a spout or minor whirlpool, which may or may not be a sign of its ever having been there.

I am, as you know, a practical man, no friend to either untested hypotheses or unwanted mysteries. They are devil-sent – or at least Roman Catholic in origin – and have few redeeming qualities. But what am I to say about some peculiar events

---

[1] This is the commentator's title. The original letter, found in the back of a logbook from Cook's ship *Endeavour*, had none. There is no indication the letter was ever posted.

which overtook us recently? What am I to say save that I am still seeking a hypothesis good enough to wash away the bitter taste of mystery?

What's more, the honourable gentlemen[2] on board – a renowned medical doctor and an even more famous scientist – are as much at a loss as I am. And they come much better equipped for this sort of thing than I do.

Let me get to the events: My crew, guests and I stepped wearily from the middle of a lashing storm, which had blown us miles off course, onto a stretch of white, trackless sand rimmed by swaying palms. Looking back out toward the ocean, there was no trace of the gale, only my bedraggled collier – sails torn and lashed – floating calmly and with ease behind a light shroud of mist. I assumed, as had happened several times before in this ocean of reversed currents, we were in the eye of the tempest and thus escaping its fury – for the moment.

As we moved cautiously up the beach, our heads swivelling back and forth, our weapons in readiness for the type of mad suicidal assault to which we had become accustomed, a group of natives stepped out from behind the palms and greeted us with gap-toothed smiles. The chief native – or the one I presumed was headman as he wore a loose white toga while the rest were naked – came forward and held out his hand for me to shake. I did not hesitate before holding my own out, knowing how quick these islanders are to take offence.[3]

[2] "The honourable gentlemen" – an obscure reference but which most scholars feel has to do with the several notables Cook was taking or had already taken to Tahiti in order to better view the movement of Venus across the sun.

[3] The misreading of native customs had more than once had near-tragic results, especially when it came to sexual practices. On several occasions, Cook had to restrain his overeager chaplain from whipping the fear of God into tangled writhing masses of flesh performing orgiastic rites in plain public view. Eventually, the chaplain learned to shut his eyes and provided the rest of the crew with blindfolds.

His hand was soft and flabby as if unused to work. And none of the natives had that gaunt, tight-fleshed appearance I had come to expect from creatures barely above subsistence level.

The headman went directly into his spiel, speaking rapidly and without pause. At first, my ear attuned to some native clucking, I did not understand what he was saying. In fact, he was speaking the King's English! Perfectly, save for a slight Highland burr. We stood there open-mouthed as he welcomed us to Paradise Island. He told us their land was ours during our visit, that we could stay for as long as we pleased and that, while on the island, we were to do nothing but rest. We know, he said pointing out toward the ocean, that it looks calm from here but yours must have been a long and terrible journey, a "passage through a watery grave."

He proved a man of his word. We were treated to a tremendous banquet during which exceedingly sweet and succulent meats were served, wrapped in minty leaves and cooked over open pits. I praised the chief on both his hospitality and his ability to speak English. He said there was nothing very astonishing about the fact. He had been born of Scottish missionary parents who had sadly suffered the consequences of their trade – martyrdom while spreading the word of God. Adopted by the tribe of rampaging natives who'd done away with his parents, he spent several years in their midst, forced to learn their ways but never forgetting the verses of the book he carried in a leather satchel: "*And it came to pass after these things, that God did tempt Abraham, and said unto him, Abraham: and he said, 'Behold, here I am'*." These and other verses he read every day, biding his time. And though the guards of the marauding tribe watched him closely – for was he not the chief's prime taboo maker? – he managed to escape one day when the men were out destroying a neighbouring tribe's fields because they had omitted a crucial step in their submission rites. Gradually, hopping from island to island, he'd made his way back to his own kind – "another missionary twosome who were the spitting image of my parents. And I ran up to them with my arms wide open, calling them my mother and father." But, though they recognized him as the long-lost son of their closest friends, they rejected him as unclean, as no longer worthy to be called a Christian. "So, in my grief, I once again went on a long journey, this time by canoe, out on the ocean itself – in the hope of being swallowed up." But, instead, he had ended up on this island, a place he now considered home.[4]

On noticing me look about, he went on to explain that the island had never gone hungry thanks to an abundance of wild game and fruit trees. Water was plentiful; the skies always blue; the seas ever warm. No wars had been fought on its soil. No earthquakes, high winds, volcanoes, or floods caused the inhabitants to shudder with fear. Everything was governed by love, the mysteries of desire, the ebb and flow of the human body.

While he talked, his voice becoming melodic and deeply resonant, my crew, guests and I gnawed away at the slabs of roast put before us. After months of dry salted meat, we sucked greedily at the sweet juices that oozed out. And then, surfeited, exhausted, with his sing-song droning in our ears, we toppled over one at a time and slept.

But I am a particularly light sleeper and many's the time when this peculiarity saved both my neck and those of the crew. On that first night on the island, I awoke to the sound of feet

---

[4] The story is considered largely apocryphal by modern historians. That the son of Scottish missionaries could have been captured by unfriendly natives is entirely possible as such things occurred on a regular basis. But nowhere save in this letter is there mention of a white chieftain and this surely would have been worth noting.

shuffling softly through the sand around me. Shadows moved in single file and disappeared into the jungle behind the outlines of a yellowish moon. I remained perfectly still, holding my pistol cocked beneath me. However, before I came fully awake, the shadows were gone. Several minutes later, as I dozed off again, there came from deep within the jungle the faint but distinct cry of animals in distress, creatures calling for help.

When I inquired of my men the next morning if they'd seen or heard anything during the night, the responses were all negative. I put it aside – a dream perhaps. After a breakfast consisting of broth from the bones we had licked clean the day before and the most delicious bananas I'd ever tasted, I satisfied myself as to the size of the tribe. At most, they numbered 100, with slightly more men than women. They lived in rickety huts on the edge of a vast jungle that occupied the entire central portion of the island.[5]

Both the men and women were plump, but in particular the women who were good-natured beyond belief. And had the unnerving habit of not only going about bare-breasted (common enough among these South Seas savages) but in many cases completely naked. This caused me to echo my standard warning to the men that whosoever touched a woman would be shot on the spot. It was disconcerting to see them turn their faces away each time a woman brought them a basket of fruit (leaning provocatively before them) or squatted down to tend the fire.

Once again that evening, we feasted on fresh meat, its succulent juices dripping through our beards and onto our laps.

---

[5] In passing but of note is the fact that Cook, a meticulous cartographer who charted among other locations parts of Labrador, New Zealand, the New Hebrides, the Hawaiian Islands and the western coast of North America, left no detailed maps of Paradise Island, nor any descriptions of its size and position. Or, if he did, they've been since lost.

When I mumbled something about our not depriving the villagers of their own rations, the chief explained that the supply of meat was more than enough for everyone. I expressed a desire to partake in one of their hunts. Or roundups. Or whatever it was they did. He said he had no objection save that they took place deep in the jungle and always at night. As well, he said that the animals, although usually tame and easy to catch, would become extremely ferocious in the presence of a strange scent.

I left it at that but, that night, spurred on by my previously mentioned hatred of mysteries, my first mate and I set out to follow the hunters into the jungle. I can say now, safe on the storm-tossed seas, that I wasn't in the least satisfied with the chief's explanations. Men don't hunt at night when the advantage is all to the prey. Nor do they sing lustily all the while. We followed at a distance of 50 yards or so. There was no danger of losing them as they stayed in single file the whole time. It occurred to me that they weren't hunting but rather heading for a predetermined spot, more like a picnic ground, it seemed, than battleground.

I was proven correct. Instead of becoming denser, less manageable, the jungle suddenly thinned out. The trees, large-trunked with tremendous crowns, reminded me of the deciduous forests back home.[6] It was at this time that we heard the first animal roar, a ghastly unearthly screech filled with sickening pain and unbearable fright. The hunters raised a cry, then loped easily between the trees as the first roar was answered by another. My mate, shivering with fear, suggested we turn back lest one of the creatures should flee our way. Or catch our scent. Pistol in hand, I ordered him on. The ominous screeches could

---

[6] Surely, Cook is mistaken here. No such forest or anything faintly resembling one has ever been reported let alone found.

now be heard almost without cease in front of us. We slowed, using the massive tree trunks to remain well-concealed.

We were almost upon the hunters when a broken plaintive sob rent the air – as if physically. It was the sort of moan that would give pause to the Lord High Executioner himself, so much sorrow and suffering did it bring in its wake. My first mate stopped, saying he would go no further. When I tried to pull him along by his coat sleeve, he broke away, stumbling backwards. I hissed for him to halt if he didn't want a ball through the back of his cowardly skull. But he paid no heed, knowing I wouldn't dare shoot for fear of alerting the others, and soon was out of sight. No matter. With nowhere to go but back to the other men, I would dish out the appropriate punishment on my return.

So I pushed on toward the screams that sent unnatural chills down my spine. They came rhythmically now, like pulses, high-pitched, wild, desperate. It seemed the hunters had surprised an entire herd of the creatures and were slaughtering them at will. But what kind of creature would just stand there and be killed? I quickened my pace, hoping to arrive before the slaughter came to an end. Ahead, I could see between the trees flames spitting into the air, coming from huge fires that formed a ring around the screams. I grew choleric, my palms sweaty, my heart pumping hot with the age-old urge to hunt, to dip my hands in the blood and drink deeply.

We are the strongest creatures on the earth, I told myself proudly. We have encircled almost all of it, using only the wind to power us and the stars to guide us. Our weapons murder from tremendous distances, raining lead on our enemies. In the future, we can only become greater, stronger, flush with even more power. The reason? We are adept at killing. Even in paradise, I told myself gleefully, even here in paradise, hunting and slaughter is necessary for survival. Oh, the meat might be more succulent and sweeter; the animals more plentiful; the kill easier. But the basic premise is the same. I began to feel at home, intimate with the place. Like the King's Own Royal Forests with the hounds foaming and red-eyed as they nipped at the belly of the fat deer brought to ground. If the first mate were before me right then, I would have shot him without a qualm, just to watch him befoul his cowardly self. And I prepared myself for the same sort of greeting from the natives the moment they discovered me.[7]

Nothing happened. I crouched behind a large tree on the edge of the fires. From there I could just make out the cages where the creatures were kept. And their shadows on the ground, rolling and tumbling over each other as if they were locked in a desperate struggle. But I couldn't see the creatures themselves as yet. In the centre of the fires, licked on all sides by the flames, was a huge slab of stone, slanted toward a sluice that ran down its front. Both the sluice and the stone were covered with blood – some caked, some still flowing. The natives slinked about, howling and hooting. One of them, naked flesh gleaming with sweat, manhood stiff before him, leapt up onto the slab and danced in an hypnotic frenzy, slapping his feet faster and faster till they were covered in blood. Then he bent down on all fours and began to lick the slab. When he looked up again, his entire face was dripping with blood. I wasn't all that surprised at what I was seeing as I had suspected something like

---

[7] Some, especially those who fancy themselves Freudians, have seen this paragraph as the start of a slow descent into paranoia and delusion. However, Captain Cook was well within his rights as a navy commander to shoot the first mate for insubordination and dereliction of duty. The fact that he realizes this bodes well for his mental state and commentators on the hunt for such things should look elsewhere for signs of illness, patterns of illogic, and collapsing mental states.

this. It was the primitives' way of dealing with the world. Or so I'd discovered in my various travels. If it rains when they dance, then naturally it is the dance that has brought the rain. Their lives are circumscribed by ritual. Nothing is done without first consulting the gods. The dancing native flipped through the air and somersaulted to the ground to a roar of approval from the others. It was then the headman came into view, distinguished always by his white robes. He stood to one side of the slab, holding a large stone axe in his hands.

There followed a flurry of activity, during which they took one of the creatures from the cage. Shadows rushed the doors but were easily driven back with sticks. The creature and its captors emerged into the glare of the fires. And then, for the first time, I saw clearly. Every bit of food I'd eaten since coming to the island, every succulent morsel, every piece of juicy leg or breast suddenly surged in my throat. Long after the last acidic dribble of undigested meat flew out of my mouth, I continued to retch, hoping perhaps to get the rest out, what was now part of my own body, my flesh and blood, part of the structure that was me. I shut my eyes so tightly they hurt. Surely a dream? I would awake on the beach. Or better still in the safety of my cabin, rocking ever so gently. Everything flickered, wavy like the flames, when I reopened them, but nothing had changed. Two of the natives, shaking like gigantic leaves, were slowly forcing down the head of a naked woman onto the slab. Her hands bound tightly behind her, she squirmed and slid side to side; her eyes were opened so wide with fear they looked to pop out of their sockets. The chief lifted the axe. I wanted to scream for them to stop; I wanted to rush out, firing my pistol; I wanted to look away. But I did nothing, transfixed as I was by the sight of the woman shivering, the axe coming down, slicing, whirring. It took two blows to separate her head, which rolled gently off the slab, rolled lazily toward me. The rest of the body, blood spurting from the neck, jerked and spasmed for several seconds, then lay still. It was only when two natives began to cut up the meat that I was able to break away.[8] My empty stomach heaving, I turned and ran, looking back only once to see another unfortunate woman being dragged to the slab.

Covered in sweat and shaking to my very boots, I broke clear of the jungle several hours later. Before me, the ramshackle village was the picture of tranquillity. A half-moon tilted in the sky; a gentle warm breeze riffled my hair; everywhere bodies lay wheezing and snoring. I was already starting to have doubts about what had happened back in the jungle when a figure detached itself from a nearby tree and headed my way. I raised my pistol when it threw itself before me and started whining: "Sir! Please, sir! I couldn't help it! I knew something awful was about to transpire." I told him he was a mongrel dog who deserved nothing better than a ball between the eyes, but he wasn't worth wasting my powder on. Then I gave him a blow to the side of the head and told him to get out of my sight. We would settle the matter once back on board. I was about to rouse my two guests as I needed other reliable witnesses when I heard movement in the jungle behind me. They were returning. I faked being asleep. The natives were once again walking single-file, each carrying a bloody slab of meat on his head. Except for the chief, who had only a large book in his hands, a book on whose cover a gentle lamb was carrying a cross.

---

[8] For the sake of historical accuracy, this grisly description has been allowed to stand as written, though the commentators would like to register a strong warning here about allowing the material to get into impressionable hands. Or in the hands of those who may use it only for the purpose of exploitation and catering to a perverted taste for the macabre.

I leaped out and, waving my pistol, confronted the headman, at the same time making enough noise to wake the others. When they saw me, they too raised their weapons. The headman stopped and smiled. "Ah, I see," he said, the picture of calmness. "You disobeyed and followed us."

"And it's lucky for me I did," I shouted. "Men! Keep your weapons at the ready. If any of these slimy excuses for human beings makes a move, you have my permission to shoot to kill."

My scientist guest came to me to ask what was the matter.

"Yes, captain," the headman said, most sweetly. "I'm most curious to know myself."

"Silence, butcher!" The men started grumbling and whispering. "Listen to me," I yelled out. "Do you know where they get the meat we've been eating? Do you know what those bloody slabs they're carrying really are?"

And I told them, calling upon the cowardly first mate to back me up – at least to the sighting of the fires. Then, in sickening detail, I described the rest. Some of the men vomited on the spot; others were in the mood to start shooting, to erase the abomination from the earth.

"No," I said. "That isn't the British way. As representatives of civilization, we must conduct ourselves according to law. A trial is necessary. A thorough investigation must be carried out. There mustn't be any reasonable doubt. That is our way and we won't let any savages undermine that. For now, round them up and keep them under guard."

During all this, neither the natives nor the headman had moved. The headman, in particular, seemed disinterested.

"Captain," he said at last after the rest of the natives had been ordered to drop their monstrous loads, "I'm truly sorry for you. For what you saw."

"You don't deny it, then?" I said, ready to jot down his every word as proof of self-incrimination.

"Deny what you saw? That would be absurd, wouldn't it?" And he shook his head, joining the rest of the native men.

The scientist suggested I lead him and the doctor back into the jungle to see the evidence of the horrible slaughter. I can't say I was enthusiastic to carry out this enterprise but felt I had little choice. So, leaving word that the natives be well-guarded, the two guests and I entered the jungle. It was remarkably beautiful in the early morning sunlight, filled with rainbow-hued orchids and birds whose tails glowed iridescent gold and purple. The events of the previous night were starting to fade into a general all-pervading mellowness when I saw the clearing and it all came back, including the lurch of my stomach.

"There it is," I said, pointing to a series of ash-mounds surrounding a smooth slab impaled by a shaft of sunlight. "The cage is gone, but they could easily dismantle it. Or drag it deeper into the jungle."

"More difficult," the scientist said, "is how they disposed of all the other proof: the bones, the flesh, the blood. Especially the blood."

"What are you talking about?" I said angrily. "The blood was everywhere. It spurted in all directions. The sluice was filled to overflowing." But there was no blood. Not the minutest drop. Perhaps they'd buried it? We turned the earth surrounding the slab. Nothing. "Heads!" I exclaimed. "Unused portions of the bodies! Intestines! They must be around here somewhere. They couldn't have rotted away so quickly." Nowhere. The jungle floor was covered by a fine mantle of grass-like material which consisted mainly of roots from the surrounding trees. It would have been easy to spot any recent digging that had been done.

"Hmm," the scientist said. "Either they have done a marvellous job of disposing of the evidence or—"

"But there *is* evidence," the doctor said.

"Of course!" I exclaimed. "Of course, there is. How utterly silly of us."

We hurried back to the village. It seemed like a tableau out of a Rococo painting: the native men sitting calmly and surrounded by my anxious sailors; the women and children off in one corner, laughing or playing quietly; the line of meat where it had been dropped. The doctor squatted down and gingerly examined a slab. He shook his head.

"This is not human. Of that, I'm sure."

I leaned back against a tree exhausted and confused. There had to be an explanation for what I'd seen. There must be. I looked about. The ship bobbed in the bay; little waves ran up the shoreline like fingers of foam; clouds as white as angels scuttled across the sky.

"Begging your pardon, Captain," said my second mate.

"Yes, what is it?"

"Sir, the headman requests permission to speak to you. Shall I bring him over?"

"Yes – No. I'll go see him." I walked over and squatted down, the eyes of every man jack there on me.

"I'm truly sorry for what you saw," the headman said softly. "It must have been horrible."

"Damn you! What did I see? Tell me. What am I supposed to have seen?"

"Why, all that you described. I see no reason for you to lie."

"But there's… there's nothing there," I sputtered, both confused and frustrated. "Save for some ash and the slab. What have you done with the blood, the bodies, the—"

The headman smiled.

"We have done nothing with them," he said. "What could we have done with them?"

"I see. That meat, then, where does it come from?"

He shrugged.

"That is something not even I know. The deep mystery at the very heart of life, perhaps. The utterly unexplainable."

"You're lying!" I screamed. "Just a lot of your primitive mumbo jumbo."

"No, Captain. There are not any lies here. This is Paradise Island."

I slammed my fist on the ground.

"Let me tell you, sir! I have travelled widely on the ocean, up and down undiscovered coasts, through ice-encrusted waterways. And everywhere I've gone I've run into those who call their land Paradise this or Paradise that – even if it came closer to a description of hell. Now, what makes you so different?"

"Nothing," he said. "Perhaps they were all telling the truth."

I stood up and laughed.

"To be honest, sir, I would like nothing better than to line you all up and shoot you – each and every last one of you. Consider it your fortune that I carry myself as a civilized man. You have done wrong. I can sense it. Smell it. The very scent fouls the air. But our laws demand hard proof and I have none." I turned to the men whom I could feel were getting restless. They needed some form of decisive action from me. "Prepare to return to ship," I said. The men cheered and set to packing.

"Would you care for some provisions?" the headman asked, a queer smile on his face. Before I knew what I was doing, I had smashed him across the side of the head with my pistol butt. Some of the natives jumped up, ready to avenge him. But the sight of my men in the kneeling position quickly calmed them down.

"Sir," I said. "You have tried my patience once too often." I turned to the doctor. "Provide him with a bandage, please."

But the headman shook his head. "There's no need. I'm uninjured."

"Do not provoke me again," I said. "Or I will be forced to drastic measures. What you do is against the tenets of even the most barbaric of apes."

"Once again my apologies," he said. "We are not all of us constituted in the same way."

"I thank the Lord on high for that."

My first mate came running up.

"Sir, we're preparing to board."

"Good," I said. "Tell Jenkins to relieve you of command. From now on he's my first mate. And thank God I don't leave you here where you belong." I turned back to the headman.

"Before I go," I said, "I would like to know one thing."

"If I can help you, I will."

"Where does your meat come from?"

He smiled. "From the slab, of course. This is, after all, Paradise Island."

I grew red and feared I'd strike him again, but held my temper.

"My good man," the scientist blurted. "Meat doesn't just appear on a slab. It must come from somewhere. That is a matter of the conservation of mass."

"And what about grace?" the headman asked.

"What!" I said. "What means grace to a slobbering bunch of cannibals who first slaughter and then eat with relish their own women?"

"I can't make you understand," he said. "I could never make you understand – not even if we talked for an eternity. Instead, may I offer—"

"If you offer us meat again," I said, jumping up, "I won't hesitate to shoot you!"

The headman laughed good-naturedly. "No, no. This is what I wish to offer you." He held out his book. "This is a Bible. But not any Bible. This belonged to my parents. I want you to take it back to England for safekeeping. I no longer need it."

I could see no reason for not accepting it, so I tucked it under my arm and climbed aboard the longboat. There was complete silence as we pushed off and the entire native tribe came down to wave goodbye: the plump men and women smiling graciously, the children holding up fistfuls of sand. As we came alongside the *Endeavour*, we found ourselves once again in the midst of a raging storm and the island vanished completely from view.

The first thing the men did when the seas settled again was to toss our meat provisions overboard. None could bear the idea of biting into flesh – even though we knew it was genuine beef from genuine British cattle and enough of it there to last us several months. I didn't object, buoyed by the fact there were plenty of places to stop along the way and load up with fruits and vegetables until our stomachs eased up a bit.

Several days out, the sea calm and the stars like jewels on a dark velvet cloth, I sat at my desk, flask of brandy at hand, to write a report of the events that had befallen us and to alert future expeditions as to the insidious nature of these islanders. It was then I noticed the headman's Bible lying where I had first placed it. For some reason unknown to me, perhaps to anchor my wandering spirit on something as solid as the word of the

Lord God, I reached for it. It was *The Holy Bible Containing the Old and New Testaments in the Authorized King James Version*. It opened naturally at Genesis 22, at a marker where some verses were underlined:

"*And they came to the place which God had told him of; and Abraham built an altar there, and laid the wood in order, and bound Isaac his son, and laid him on the altar upon the wood.*

"*And Abraham stretched forth his hand, and took the knife to slay his son.*

"*And slew him.*"[9]

You understand, then, why we turned around, why we must search for this Paradise Island and not yield until we find it, not give up until we once more have it in our sights. You do understand, don't you?

Your Faithful Servant
Captain James Cook
Aboard *H.M.S. Endeavour*

---

[9] As the particular Bible of which Capt. Cook speaks has never been found, this must be considered a simple misreading of the original text. Another possibility, though a remote one, is that the family of the headman had its own Bible printed with the words deliberately altered. At any rate, Cook himself never had occasion to mention anything about the island except in this letter. Nor did those who sailed with him. This may be understandable in the light that they all partook of the flesh, even if involuntarily, and thus felt it necessary to close the incident. On the other hand, fabrication, in total or in part, can't be discounted out of hand.

# CASEBOOK: IN THE MATTER OF FATHER DANTE LAZARO

## A. THE CASE FOR BEATIFICATION

[*My fellow members of the Galactic Curia: As Chief Investigator for the Interplanetary Commission on Beatification Candidacies, I have been asked by His Extreme Holiness Pope Aldebaran V, Head of the Holy Roman Catholic Church (Trans-Universal), to check into the status of one of our most illustrious and intrepid foot soldiers in the never-ending battle against ignorance and paganism. I'm referring, of course, to Father Dante Lazaro, the first priest from the One True Church to make direct contact with an alien species. Now, I could go on ad infinitum, narrating tales of Father Lazaro and his incredible exploits. But I felt it would be best to have Father Lazaro tell his own story in this matter. So, it is thus with extreme pride that I present as evidence these two transmissions to the Committee – and to recommend, on the basis of these same transmissions, that procedures be started immediately for the beatification of Father Lazaro. Alone and light years from home, he died a brave martyr for his cause. Beatification is the least we can do to recognize his courage in thought and deed.*]

## Transmission #1

(Encoded transmission, hyperspace trajectory classified)

Dateline: Planetfall, New Horizon, Capella, Auriga

From: Father Dante Lazaro, voluntarily commissioned to serve as chaplain on the Zodiac Defender, Scout Ship Second Class

To: Pope Aldebaran IV

Subject: On the Successful Propagation of the Faith in Advance of Colonization

Your Extreme Holiness:

It should please you immensely to learn that, within weeks of our making initial contact with the Indigenous population (thank God, at last a species with whom we can communicate, even if only on the most primitive terms), the Christianization of New Horizon has succeeded beyond our wildest expectations. And, by Christianization, I mean specifically the rites of the Trans-Universal Roman Catholic Church as it alone among the multitude of sects, cults and other religious deviations on the Zodiac Defender has managed thus far to get a foothold.

To begin with, no one on that dismal day of arrival – when mother ship first settled on the lowland bowl we have come to call home – could have envisioned a more stunning victory or such a rapid change in the outlook of these creatures. Faith, if given the least opportunity, will indeed conquer all time and distance. The power of the Church is shown once again in its ability to span parochial differences and to dig beyond superficial dissimilarities to get right to the heart of the matter. Or should I say its spirit?

Not that it wasn't a struggle, the most difficult part being to convince our own commanders and tacticians. As usual, they had but one solution to any problem that might arise: arm to the teeth; make the perimeter secure for ourselves; and then negotiate peace. When that fails, show them examples of our firepower, subjugate them and claim it all for the Federation. Except that the Indigenous population was in no mood to bow without a fight. And this was the situation, the sides drawn up and ready to annihilate one another – we with superior weaponry, they stocked with practically inexhaustible man-power – when I decided it was time to act.

Dressed in my finest, most ornate gold vestments and with the Host held on high as my only weapon, I emerged from the ship – against the wishes of the so-called experts, religious and lay, I might add – and walked toward the creatures who huddled snarling and hissing behind a small series of hillocks. About halfway there, I stopped, placed the chalice on a flat rock and then returned to the ship. It took several minutes before one of the creatures trotted out into the open and, with a motion too quick for the human eye, ingested the Host. He then squatted down and produced a fist-sized crystal before wandering back to the others.

Now, as I write, converts to the Trans-Universal Roman Catholic Church (*extra orbim terrarum*) are filing past our makeshift altars by the thousands. We barely have time to repli-cate and consecrate the Hosts before they are snapped up in their powerful yet reverential jaws. And we must forgive them the unorthodoxy of licking, chewing and sucking rather than swallowing whole. You must admit it's truly a minor point when their faces glow with the knowledge that the body and blood of Christ now flow through them.

They are so fervent, in fact, that we must guard against them sneaking back into line for a second helping. But it must be attributed to a praiseworthy enthusiasm. For are they not like unto the children of God poised on their hind legs, tiny fore-claws clasped in prayer, tail jerking spasmodically, the light at last shining through their yellow, unblinking eyes? And, while the representatives of the other major religions have also set up their booths, public confessionals, information centres, singa-longs, and sacred places (and even a healing lodge), they've yet to attract one single recruit.

As well, it should please you no end to know that the experts mentioned above – the sociologists, psychiatrists, ethnologists, planetologists, etc. (all with "exo-" before their titles) – sent here to study and "civilize" these creatures are in a tizzy. They com-plain to the Captain that we've usurped their authority, have introduced messy anthropomorphic ideas about personal salva-tion and idol worship to displace their offer of clean, pure athe-ism. But the Captain is interested only in results and will do nothing to jeopardize the production of those crystals, which turn out to be a by-product of the creatures' spiritual bliss.

Like the fabled early Christians, these new converts are mil-itant in their faith. Their zeal, their enthusiasm, their spirit put us to shame. Heaven, I'm sure, will soon have a new set of mar-tyrs with which to contend. These are the devout creatures who think nothing of sacrificing themselves to bring Christ to the high, jagged mountains where the more ferocious, the less civi-lized among them still live, carnivores who, I'm told, will resort to eating one another when nothing else is available.

(Here, the distinctions between the "lowland" creatures and the "highlanders" must be noted. The lowlanders have devel-oped a form of domestication, herds of "cattle" – six-legged, rainbow-coloured creatures with one spiral horn – which they tend for food. The highlanders, on the other hand, are roving packs of hunters, downing and devouring whatever crosses their paths. As for the vegetation on the planet, in the form of fuzzy purple "trees" that grow to a height of several metres, only the "cattle" seem capable of ingesting it. Within the first few days of our landing, we witnessed one case where a young creature accidentally swallowed a leaf. Almost immediately, he began to writhe in agony. Rather than await the horrific, lingering death sure to follow, he reached down with a sharp claw and disembowelled himself right before our eyes.)

So what better proof of the converts' faith, pray tell, can there be than the fact that, after these poor souls have been torn apart and devoured completely, their attackers – smacking lips and trailing gore – also find themselves converted? And they too join the long lines marching toward the lowlands, eyes gleaming with the light of God.

It is a sight to strike awe into even the most jaded space veteran and certainly one to warm your heart, Your Extreme Holiness, should you ever have occasion to find yourself in this sector.

Postscriptum:
As per your standing orders on these matters, we have made discreet enquiries into the Church's claim to a fair share of the crystals. The Captain, of course, shrugs, saying she's but a simple soldier and ill-equipped to make such decisions. According to her, questions of jurisdiction must be solved by high-level negotiation – back on Earth. She's right naturally, but I would feel much better if she hadn't immediately claimed them for the Federation and placed them under strict military embargo.

In any case, now that Your Extreme Holiness has been made aware of the situation, there's no doubt you will act upon the knowledge. I will be happy to send you any further documentation you may need.

## Transmission # 2

(Encoded transmission, trajectory classified)
Dateline: New Horizon, one year after planetfall
From:    Father Lazaro
To:    Pope Aldebaran IV
Subject:   On Blessed Lizard Philopater – Necessary Progress in the Propagation of the Faith

Your Exalted and Most Infallible Holiness:

With your permission, we are in the first stages of an application to have one of the creatures beatified. This in the hope that a few decades down the line (speed is of the essence) sainthood will follow. Proof of his achievements, along with his remains, are being expedited (in triplicate naturally) to the Interplanetary Commission on Beatification Candidacies. As well, we have applied for a Devil's Advocate to make his way here as soon as possible. Rest assured, this creature's deeds will stand any amount of scrutiny. And those who attest to his worthiness say that he is fit to be compared favourably to the bloodied martyrs of the pre-trans-galactic era. I hope you'll agree once you've been made aware of his deeds.

For what had begun as child's play, the creatures' falling over themselves to be converted and then rushing off to convert others, soon turned out to be somewhat of an illusion – much to the delight of our mortal enemies, the Zen Buddhists Martian Faction. It was discovered, for example, that most if not all of the creatures were attracted to our religion simply because the Host served to stimulate them much as hallucinogens once did us. Whether these are genuine religious ecstasies or not is a theological point for the Curia. Suffice it to say that what we mistook for mystic states in the presence of Our Lord amounted to little more than drug-induced stupors.

It embarrasses me to say that the "chemical" experts on board took this as a good sign, as a way to control the natives without having to resort to armed intervention. At any rate, it seems that, when the creatures had had their fill of the Host (often not bothering to wait for the blessing and instead partaking in kamikaze raids on the factories where they were produced), many of them returned to the mountains and resumed the old ways of life. This included unceasing war, cruelty, cannibalism and all the other evils associated from time immemorial with unbridled paganism and wrong-headed cultism (not to mention our own misguided liberalization programs stemming back to Paul of Damascus).

Reports reaching us had them once again taking up the worship of blood-stained gods, offering their own and others' limbs as sacrifices. In fact, we have reliable information of a horrendous ritual whereby the first-born, on coming of age (distinguished by certain patterns on the tail), devours the still-twitching flesh of his progenitors.

The first hints of trouble came about two months after planetfall, in the hastily built classrooms where the younger creatures were being taught a simple catechism and liturgy. They possess remarkable memories and soon the schools were filled with the guttural sounds of "Ave Marias" and "Pater Nosters" being machine-translated back and forth between our language and theirs.

Everything seemed to be going along fine until one of the teachers – urged on by the psychiatrist, I believe – decided to try a little experiment. He withheld the morning's ration of Hosts. By afternoon, all was chaos. The ground ran red with blood. Not that they touched any of us, mind you. Nevertheless, it wasn't the most pleasant of sights to see one creature scuttle by with another half-swallowed, its legs still kicking piteously, something seemingly directly out of Hieronymus Bosch.

The troops managed to calm things down the same day by depositing large quantities of Hosts at various intervals around the ship while I used the skimmer to hover overhead and bless these mounds. Soon, the creatures were blissful once again, quietly licking their lips and squatting to expel more crystals. The psychiatrist was reprimanded and would have received a more severe punishment if I hadn't intervened. After all, I said, one must have patience with someone who tries to do good, even if he uses outmoded methods and questionable psychology under the panoply of misguided atheism.

Still, this couldn't go on. The psychiatrist had done nothing but bring things to a head. We didn't have the facilities nor the time to go on producing Hosts at the rate they were being devoured. Our chemists tried ersatz wafers. These were immediately spit out. Other drugs were replicated but these too had no effect on the creatures. They swallowed LSD by the gallon; heroin, the designer drugs, PCP, angel dust, ecstasy, the latest concoctions from the sands of Pluto – nothing. They just kept eating the Hosts – and producing crystals. Crystals! Your Holiness, they're everywhere. Thousands of them. One can't turn over in bed without feeling a sharp edge. The Captain has magnanimously offered to lift the military embargo to allow us to store some in our quarters. As a sign of her good faith and trust, she said. I told her there was no hope for it. She then begged to impose on our charity.

I digress, for what happened next can best be described as a miracle. That morning, several weeks after the first eruption, the Captain called a meeting to which I, as senior religious representative, was invited. The gist was that the production of Hosts was to be cut back to normal so that other ship business could be carried out. Some – the sociologist and the psychiatrist in particular – argued for a total cut-off but that only showed how far they'd allowed their emotions to cloud their thinking. I pointed out mildly some Hosts would still be needed. There were sheepish grins all around. In any case, the vote was unanimous. All we could do now was brace ourselves and make sure there was as little loss of life as possible.

The plan was to be set in motion the next morning and Capella arose much like Sol would back home, casting its yellowish light on the tiny purple trees surrounded by grazing cattle, the hunched-over creatures in the last throes of Host-ecstasy, the mother ship gleaming in tranquillity. But it was a false tranquillity. The entire base was on maximum alert. There were even contingency plans for a quick blast-off in case the creatures decided to turn on what could be perceived as the source of their torment.

One by one, all across the plain, they stirred, shook themselves awake, yawned, rubbed sleep from their eyes. It's amazing, Your Holiness, how much they looked – when the light hit them a certain way – just like any other sheep in the Lord's flock. One by one they made their way to where the Hosts normally awaited them. And then, not finding them, stood around in confusion. Soon, the grumbling started; eyes flashed red against the slanting light; claws reached out to push others aside, to bat away the smaller, less powerful ones. This was it. Any moment they would begin to devour each other.

But, just when the situation looked most grim, when my own faith was being shaken to the core, when it seemed that all our work had been for naught, there was a loud roar in the distance and the creature we would come to know as Blessed Lizard Philopater trotted up in a cloud of dust. Judging from his appearance he was a young, strong male in the prime of life but that certainly wouldn't have been sufficient cause for the others to halt what they were doing (except perhaps to consider him as food). What really got their attention was the fact he was carrying a large purple branch in his mouth. And he was slowly chewing on it. They gasped in unison. Why wasn't he ripping at his own intestines, writhing in agony? No, he just chewed calmly and smiled as if he saw something other than a desolate landscape on a primitive planet.

And then, sitting in their midst, he told his story. By this time, the psychiatrist, myself and several of the other religious leaders had ventured out of the ship. As luck would have it, I had brought my translator-recorder with me and was able to tape what Blessed Lizard Philopater said verbatim (copy enclosed with present transmission):

"My fellow People. It was as a child that I first journeyed – one among thousands – to the altar of the featherless, yet odoriferous, bipeds. There to partake in the eating of the sacred Host, the gift they brought to the People. But, unlike many who, crazed by the taste, stayed in the lowlands, my family returned to the mountains to resume our previous way of life. It was thus I spent my Childhood and grew up as a normal Person, taking part in the ceremonies that have been ours since time immemorial. And thus I would have continued if an extraordinary event hadn't taken place upon my reaching Manhood. For, when the rites of passage were being prepared and offered unto me well-oiled and sweetened, I refused. (There was a collective gasp at this point, translated by the machine as a reaction to an utterance so blasphemous there were no words for it.) Yes, I refused. I would not touch a single scale on my Father's body. Though he hissed at me and spat in my face, though my Mother wept with rage and went about ripping flesh from her chest to throw at me, I refused. I would rather do violence to myself, I said, than eat my Father. I would rather cut off my foreclaws than taste the flesh of my Mother. For, was it not They who had brought me forth? And so I was driven away from the Community, cursed with the sign that my flesh was unclean – and a warning to all that certain death followed upon eating me. It was thus I wandered about the forest becoming more and more lonely, torn bitterly between thoughts of my Family and the certainty that I'd done right. And out of the deepest despondency, out of the knowledge that the only escape lay in death, I tore a branch from the nearest tree and stuffed it into my mouth. I should've died, you say. I should've writhed miserably, beating my tail in anguish. I should've vomited up all my sins. Well, I did writhe and beat my tail. And I did vomit. And I even saw the Great Father coming for me, claws outstretched gently before Him. But I didn't die. For here I am before you, and I bring good news."

There was grumbling when he held out the branch. Some of the elders openly doubted and were all for holding a general council to decide what to do. But one of the younger females sprang forward and had half the branch in her mouth before any of the others could react. (In passing, it should be stated, Your Holiness, that the designation of male-female is purely arbitrary on our part. Males we call those with primary sexual characteristics resembling ours; females those with a lack of visible sexual characteristics. None have ever been examined. Nor have any ever been seen engaging in recognizable sexual activity.) That was the catalyst. Soon, a large number of the younger creatures were chewing away without any convulsions or other ill-effects.

Naturally, everyone had their own explanation for what had happened. The sociologist claimed it was a natural development in their social order, analogous to grasshoppers becoming locusts given the right stimuli; the biologist speculated that the ingesting of the Hosts had somehow altered their metabolism; the psychiatrist made noises about mass hypnosis and the id's conquest by the superego; the planetologist put the blame on us for interfering without first doing the proper case studies; the Martian Faction Zen Buddhist made inexplicable noises and said he understood. The Captain let them fight it out, caring as she did only that the creatures had stopped covering the planet with crystals, thus upholding the value of those already in our possession. I said nothing, Your Holiness, knowing full well it was a miracle, the first of many to be attributed to Blessed Lizard Philopater.

For, when his work was finished in the lowlands and the creatures had been converted to peace-loving herbivores who came to church on Sunday and offered their prayers to God, he returned to the mountains. I remember well the day he first spoke to me of this. He was sitting on a low mound, the height of calmness, flicking out his tongue to taste the air.

"This is all very wonderful," he said. "The things about me finally start to make sense. From the tiniest grain of sand to the incalculably immense explosions of supernovae, there's a meaning to it. A purpose and a reason. Isn't that so?"

I nodded, as always mesmerized and awed when in the over-powering shadow of his presence.

"Then, perhaps, you can tell me why I'm not satisfied? Perhaps you can explain why I wake up in the middle of the night to the sound of voices in despair, to voices calling me from far away?" I started to say something, but he held up his foreclaw. "Ah, but I know the answer already."

The answer was that he felt he hadn't yet completed his ministry, that there were things still to be done in the mountains where, unseen, the old brutalities went on unchecked, a reminder that not all was sweetness and light. Worse still, it served as a strong tug to the converted who had the occasional urge to take up the old ways, the idea of so-called simple ways.

And so, despite all attempts to dissuade him, he went back. Everyone knew it probably meant his death. What else could explain the thousands who followed him to the edge of the cliffs and watched him disappear from sight in a silence that defied even ordinary breathing, in a stillness that had Capella herself frozen for a moment in the sky?

That was several months ago, and we heard nothing more of him until a week ago when one of the creatures came stumbling half-dead from the mountains. He was suffering from numerous lacerations and wounds and most of the time mumbled incoherently, but what we were able to get out of him wasn't encouraging. He told a horrible tale of torture, mutilation and depravity. Apparently, Blessed Lizard Philopater and a number of foothill converts had penetrated to the very heart of the old country, to the place where the deepest mysteries were kept, protected by the most ferocious and unthinking guardians, the Blind Acolytes of the Pit. Most of Philopater's group was quickly dispatched. Philopater himself, however, was accorded no such honour.

Instead, he was being kept as a living food source. The moment a limb grew back, it was torn off and eaten before his very eyes, accompanied by the mocking words of his own creed: "Who, the day before He suffered, took bread into His holy and venerable hands, and having raised His eyes to heaven, unto Thee, O God…"

You must forgive me, Your Extreme Holiness, for the anger I felt when I heard these words, the utter blasphemy in them. In the fury of the moment, I armed myself and, rising above the land with a skimmer, made my way to the spot where the creature indicated Philopater was being tortured. Fortunately for me the fiends quickly scattered when they saw the skimmer. Else I might, in my unthinking rage, have blasted the lot of them. (Yes, Your Holiness, my confessor has given me appropriate penance.) The sight of Philopater, however, was enough to bring even a Galactic mining overlord to tears. Here was the kindest, gentlest, most selfless creature in the universe reduced to a bloody stump, covered in ooze, frothing and foaming and writhing with pain, a pain no other could have endured. He looked at me like someone already halfway to a better place. And smiled.

"Ah, Father Lazaro. There was one with your name many eons ago who arose from the dead, wasn't there?"

I nodded, speechless, unable to stem the tears.

"So it's only the start of the journey."

Mercifully, God took him then. After administering Extreme Unction, I dragged his body to the skimmer and flew back to the lowlands. There, he was covered in my gold vestments and exposed for all to see. The plan was to keep him that way until putrefaction began to set in. That usually took less than three days under Capella. But, after a week during which thousands walked past, his body still didn't show any signs of decay.

It was then that I decided to send his remains to the Interplanetary Commission on Beatification Candidacies with the hope that he would be looked upon with favour. I believe I have made the right decision in this matter, even if I do feel presumptuous in doing so – but the final ruling is obviously up to you.

*[Fellow members of the Galactic Curia: This was the last message we received from Father Lazaro, even though the rest of the New Horizon colony continued to transmit up to 20 years ago. At that point, all communications stopped. We must await the imminent arrival of the second wave of colonizers for further word.]*

## B. THE DEVIL'S ADVOCATE

### Transmission #1
(Encoded transmission, trajectory classified. Strict security at level 10: For the Pope's Eyes Only.)

Dateline: New Horizon, 35 years after original planetfall.

From: Monsignor Seirizzin, Special Papal Investigator for the Examination of Beatification Candidates

To: Pope Aldebaran V

Subject: On the Decision on Whether or Not to Proceed with Beatification for Father Dante Lazaro

Your Extreme Holiness:

When I first set out on this trip, it was considered a mere formality – and I was prepared to present only a perfunctory rebuttal to the beatification process for Father Dante Lazaro.

After all, I told myself, he was a simple man who may not have done things strictly by the book – but he always did them from the unbounded goodness of his heart and from his concern for the welfare of others: a perfect exemplar for the more innocent folk who need that type of simplicity amid life's complexities. Now that I have arrived on New Horizon, I remain of the same opinion – at least officially. However, there are a few details I wish to clear up just for my own satisfaction.

As was suspected – and feared – from their 20-year silence, the worst has come to pass. There is little remaining of that original scouting mission. All the Federation inspectors have found are the burned-out hulk of the Zodiac Defender and a few blasted building sites. And, inside the Zodiac Defender were what we must assume are the charred remains of the crew. At first, we couldn't tell if this was the lot of them – but a close count of the body parts and an examination of the original logbooks revealed that one person was missing. Or, at least, so we thought. We were later to discover that there were actually two bodies not accounted for. This should have gladdened our spirits – perhaps they were still alive. But a cursory inspection of the planet's surface showed us that, without a miracle, there was little chance of survival away from the mother ship.

A check of the buildings revealed that they had been blasted by an unceasing barrage of laser fire. Exercising my prerogative as a diplomat extraordinaire for the Vatican, I immediately placed a seal on what had been Father Lazaro's sleeping quarters and office.

And a good thing, too – for it is what I found inside that has left me somewhat perplexed if not disturbed. As you will see, the most important evidence consists of (a) a note in Father

Lazaro's private diary and (b) three high security hyperspace transmissions which he prepared but never sent.

Here then is the note, written sometime after Father Lazaro's final transmission a year after planetfall:

"To my God – I will most likely be condemned to the everlasting tortures of hell for this – but I must get it off my chest. I didn't quite tell the whole truth when I set out for his Extreme Holiness Pope Aldebaran IV the tragic circumstances under which Blessed Lizard Philopater met his end. In short, he didn't expire under torture. I killed him. Even though against both Your law and my own conscience, it was the only humanitarian thing to do. He pleaded with me the whole time to put an end to his misery; he begged me not to let him suffer any longer; he ordered me to destroy him before he undid all the good work he'd achieved. And so, may You forgive me, I finally did as he asked. If the Beatification Commission had taken the trouble to examine thoroughly the remains of Blessed Lizard Philopater, they would have found a pinprick just behind the tiny earhole on the left-hand side of his head. It is there that I inserted the needle tipped with poison, a needle which ironically I pilfered from the psychiatrist who was prepared to do himself in as a last resort."

Of course, the Commission never did examine the body closely at the time as it had absolutely no intention of granting this creature beatification. The absurdity of the idea is beyond discussion and it was never even brought up. As well, there is the question of whether or not the "assisted suicide" of this creature would actually constitute a sin on the part of Father Lazaro. I would argue not in that the laws, for the moment at least, apply only to fellow human beings.

More disturbing are the three transmissions Father Lazaro prepared but never sent. The first is dated at about five years after planetfall; the second 10; and the third 15. Why he hadn't transmitted them in the first place should become fairly obvious the moment you read them. Here they are, then:

A:

An extraordinary series of events has taken place over the last few days. First, a delegation of elders requested a meeting with the ship's council during which they announced they were leaving. Questioned on what they meant; they could give no further explanation. The following morning, the makeshift city was literally quivering with activity as the creatures and their herds prepared to move out. By nightfall, it was empty, the last stragglers silently winding their way into the mountains. A reconnaissance skimmer sent to track them returned with the news that there was no sign of them, that they'd simply vanished – most likely into the thousands of caves that dotted the higher hillsides.

Before we even had time to come to grips with this strange turn of events, something else happened to make us forget our sudden abandonment: Peculiar movements were detected in the ship's hold. The crystals were stirring. It's definitely a growth pattern, was the way the biologist put it. Are you trying to say – the Captain blurted out. Yes, Ma'am. These crystals are eggs. But that's not possible, the sociologist said. They seem to be a one-time thing. Surely, this can't be their reproductive mechanism. They reproduce any way they want, the psychiatrist answered. That's right, the biologist continued. Just another way to make sure.

In any case, the crystals were cracking open and would surely die of suffocation if left piled in the storage areas. We organized work crews to get them out into the open, to put them down where the sun could warm them. We had barely finished when they began to change shape, to go from crystalline formations to organic ones. And soon we had hundreds of newly minted creatures on our hands and the Captain cursing under her breath, muttering that after all this time the planet had taken back the only worthwhile thing it had given us.

I told her we should look on the bright side. Judging from their first attempts at foraging, this new batch seemed to be born herbivores and displayed none of the aggressive characteristics of their forebears. But she had other things on her mind. Obviously, the presence of the crystals had been high on her list of the planet's selling points for eventual colonization. That was her problem, however. Mine was to see to the education of these brand new souls.

**B:**

I have resisted the onslaught as long as I could but now I find myself totally alone in this, with little support from the others, some of whom would dearly love to see the Church discomfited if not humiliated. My dear Father Lazaro, the psychiatrist whines, how does it feel to be beaten at your own game? He is the nastiest of the lot but, at least, he is open about it. The others smirk and giggle – especially the so-called "religious leaders." It is, however, no laughing matter. For what should have been the Church's crowning glory has turned into its worst debacle since... since... There's no point holding back – since the Fall of Constantinople.

The new batch of creatures are all we had hoped for: intelligent, quick to learn (they now speak our language perfectly while our linguists are still struggling with the basics of theirs), sensitive and, above all, caring. So why is it that the Church is caught in a massive retreat? Why is it we are being outflanked by our own weapons? Why is it I can hardly leave the ship without being accosted by one of the creatures anxious to speak, to ask questions, to probe? I've thought of complaining formally to the Captain, but she is much preoccupied these days with the raising of her own child (the eggs stimulated fertility in many unexpected quarters, Your Extreme Holiness). Besides, what exactly would I complain about?

The truth of the matter, Your Extreme Holiness, is that the creatures learn too well. It's hard to believe that, barely 10 terrestrial years ago, their culture was on a par with ours when we first emerged from the dim caves of Earth. Now, they devour information faster than we can provide it. There is always a long waiting list to use the computer library terminals. And their questions become harder and harder to answer. Not only that but I have begun to detect a note of mockery, of gentle cynicism in their phrasing.

"Query: Could you please inform us as to the nature of sainthood procedures? Is there a minimum number of miracles, for example? Does the Church award sainthood on a percentage basis: population, level of sanctity, skin colour, number of claws, etc.? Do you see the difference between the number of saints on mother ship – which has one for each day of the year (with minor ones having to double and triple up) – and our own planet (with nary a one) as a reflection of the ship's infinitely more vast degree of holiness? Could slight changes in gravitational fields, for example, have an effect on sainthood? Or time warps perhaps?"

And that is only one example. Can you imagine thousands sending in similar queries? Not only that but, thanks to highly developed imaginations, many of the creatures are starting to fill in what they perceive as blanks in our liturgy and mythology. When I wasn't able to answer a question on the physical make-up of the Lord (I couldn't very well give Him a purely human aspect, now could I?), they took it as licence to create Him in their own image. He can be seen at this very moment sitting at the right claw of the Almighty. To make the confusion complete, Jesus now bears a striking resemblance to Blessed Lizard Philopater.

Most ominous of all, some have begun to question the logic of our basic tenets: the Trinity, the Resurrection, Virgin Birth, etc. When I explain to them that these must be taken on faith, they nod – and ask the same questions again. Sometimes, I suspect the psychiatrist and the Zen Buddhist are behind it all for they have always been jealous of our success here and take any opportunity to undermine our work. But there's nothing I can do in the absence of proper inquisition methods.

In any case, it would be extremely helpful if you could provide me with some officially sanctioned answers to these questions – or at least with an official way to deal with them. This isn't for my sake, of course, as my faith is unshakable, but for that of the thousands of souls whom we may lose to cynicism and doubt. Or, worse still, to one of the other religions poised like vultures to scoop up the fallen. After all, it's not like this is the first time we have faced this problem. Nor will it likely be the last. But I urge you to hurry, Your Extreme Holiness. Time is running very short. The Age of Doubt is almost upon us. Again.

C:

I long for the simple, the miraculous, the take-it-on-faith. I long for those early days of Host frenzy and Saint Lizard Philopater (he must be a saint by now). But that's no longer possible. The tomes are growing by the day, spewing continuously out of the computer's jaws, becoming so weighty they threaten to crush us all. The questions are piling up – unanswered; unanswerable. We have laboured night and day, day and night for close to 15 years. And what has it got us? What exactly have we achieved?

Forgive me, your Extreme Holiness. Forgive me. I have become a St. Paul in reverse. By the time help arrives, I fear that I will be long gone, fleeing backwards along the road into Damascus. The tight lid of my faith has been pried wide open. And they are crawling in now one at a time, cramming themselves into what was once an unbreachable sanctuary. And each and every one demands the truth from me, demands what I can no longer deliver…

Dead. Dead. They are all dead. No, not all. I have with me the child, the Captain's child. We two are all that's left of the original expedition. It had to be done. They stood in the way – the captain, the psychiatrist, the Zen Buddhist, the planetologist, the biologist. Their laughter had become too much, haunting even my dreams. From my earliest days in the seminary, gazing out at the Martian sun, I have been taught one thing. It has been ingrained in me: When the possibility of conversion is reduced to zero, one must resort to other methods – and even the most drastic are condoned for the greater glory of God and the Trans-Universal Roman Catholic Church. It was a simple thing as all of them insisted on staying aboard the mother ship. But, fear not. I committed their souls to God. It was a simple thing…

There is nothing left for me here. I must cut my losses. I'm sure you understand, Your Extreme Holiness. The creatures have retreated into the mountains once more, into the deadly crags where my beloved Saint Lizard Philopater met his fate. Before me stands the burned-out ship, very unphoenix-like. I have ringed the factories of the Host, the makeshift classrooms, the de-consecrated church grounds with self-firing lasers. They will melt back into the ground. Then, the child and I will also go into the mountains. She is the only one I have been able to rescue.

Her mind is young and pliable, receptive to the tenets of the true faith. Together, we will spread the word. The Liturgy According to Saint Lizard Philopater. Nothing else matters. Nothing else could matter. For truth is not an argument upon ecclesiastical niceties, is it? No, truth is like a sharpened fore-claw, ready to cut short any debate, to bring things to their foregone and preordained conclusion. Once you have looked upon it, nothing else is left in the range of your vision. Perhaps, someday, you too will be fortunate enough, Your Extreme Holiness, to experience…

*[And so it ends. But the danger of repercussions for the Trans-Universal Roman Catholic Church has only just started, as Your Extreme Holiness is well aware. While I agree that the note and these transmissions should be placed in the proto-Vatican vaults, it is my recommendation that they be sealed in perpetuity. Officially, I am in total agreement with the Federation investigators who have concluded that the first expedition to New Horizon met its fate at the hands of intractably hostile creatures who managed to turn our own weapons against us. As for Father Lazaro, the investigators conclude he was taken away against his own will when the creatures retreated to their mountain fortresses. And there he was tortured, killed and eaten — along with the Captain's unfortunate child who, let us pray, underwent baptism before her sorry end.*

*With that in mind, this Devil's Advocate has no choice but to put in the highest recommendation for immediate beatification for Father Dante Lazaro. All personal doubts and opinions aside, it is the only logical thing we can do, the only way not to risk a complete debacle. I'm sure you will agree, Your Extreme Holiness, once you have had time to fully consider it.]*

# THE MOTHER

The corruption smashed, you hold its grub, ginger-lightly, in your jaws. The black head, helpless and blind without a protective coat of flesh, twists and squirms, looking for escape, for a way to dig itself back into the elemental jacket. But you squeeze its thoracic segment just right – just so – firm enough to keep it from writhing free but not so hard as to puncture the skin, to cause the bitter yellow juices to come squirting down your own throat. This is a delicate balancing act you've performed many times before at the edge of the wood: the crush of the gas-bloated carcass, eviscerated and fetid; the frenzied scuttling of its squatter's-rights inhabitants; the quick dip, twist and scoop of your paw; the gentle, almost tender, deposit into your mouth of the wriggling larva.

It's at the edge of the wood that you always find these carcasses, the ones who couldn't quite make it to cover, to the safety of dense green canopy. There, behind you, lies the city, supremely unsafe now, filled with the giant things that beat black wings, that burn and scorch with a single flash of their eyes. You have washed away all memories of that particular place, have supplanted them with a cicatrix whose healing power is a lack of remembrance. Nostalgia is dangerous, especially now. It cuts the connections to the hindbrain, makes decisions a matter of emotion or thought rather than necessity. You know that instinctively and instinctively turn to head into the wood.

Besides, that's where your child waits, does it not? Smuggled from a warm bed moments before the giant-winged ones came roaring in to claim it for themselves, peeling back the building from the top a floor at a time in search of you, of your child. In the end, the building itself resembled an animal that had been gutted – except that entities called your friends, your family, your neighbours were those spilled guts. Friends? Family? Neighbours? What do those words mean?

You escaped through a basement door that led out beyond the garage – do you remember that? – the exit sign shattered but miraculously still flashing red when everything else around it had gone dead. And the creatures pursued you through the streets, relentless, as you dodged between cars that idled but would not run. You ran, though, didn't you, the child in your arms wrapped in a Thinsulate blanket?

Everything whispered "hopeless" to you – from the toasters frozen in mid-pop to the sizzling jolts of electricity that shot skyward like reverse lightning. Everything said to come to your senses, to give them what they wanted, to let go. But you couldn't let go, could you? You had to keep running – even though you had nothing left to give, even though the air came out of you in explosive gulps that only barely managed to keep the blood pumping, the legs in motion. And just as you were about to drop, to throw yourself like a fleshy shield over your child, their pursuit stopped. Mewling and angry, lashing out in frustration, they pulled back, for some reason unable to go beyond a certain point on the perimeter of the city. As if all their power and energy came from that megalopolis, that matrix of unplanned connections. As if they were helpless without direct contact with its myriad formulae, its intricate scalar webbing, its slow-running rivers of human sludge.

How long did you sleep then? Do you remember? It must have been a very long time, a time that proved beyond your ability to count. When you awoke, you were no longer the same. That much you sensed. It seemed that one thing and one thing alone held your attention – the survival of your child, i.e. its careful hiding and feeding. Everything else had grown outside your ever-thickening skin, had broken all ties with you.

Where once you knew addition and the stars, now there roamed only charred and misfiring voltages; where once the watering of willowy plants spelled "God" so clearly and invincibly that doubt was impossible, now remained only a chilling obsession. A foregone conclusion. But it must be that way for you to outlast them. Nothing else must matter. The least mote in your eye could mean the end, could cause you to bite too hard. Or to let go entirely, allowing the grub to wiggle back into the decay, the mucinous packages that signified food between muscle and bone.

And so, good mother that you are, you lope off in the direction where your child awaits. You can envision it now, safe and warm under its thick covering of leaves: mouth open, tiny hands waving, the hushed tinkle of bells on its feet, a sound only you can hear. You stop for a moment, just out of range, to lift your head and sniff the air. At the first hint of danger, you'll veer off. You'll thrash and make as much noise as possible, leading predator away from prey – like a good mother should. Like any good mother would. And you'll only return when it's safe, when the voracious ones have turned on each other to create more carcasses and more grubs. But, this time, everything is calm.

The earth isn't rumbling; the sky has no shadows; the darkness stays on the horizon until its proper time has come; the hushed bells tinkle. Only the grub wriggling between your lips reminds you of what you must do.

And so you reach down, anxious to brush away the disguising leaves, to touch once again that which gives essence to your existence. It is a greedy little thing and its black, reflectionless eyes light up when it sees the grub. You bring your face down to it, shaking your head. It arches toward you, mouth snapping, fingers opening and closing convulsively. Rigid with fear, sensing its fate, the grub tries for the last time to escape, to pull back. But the gesture is in vain. You release it for a moment's freedom. And it tumbles, falling end over end. One swallow, one hurried gulp brings it into your child's endless throat.

You rise again. The rictus of a smile flashes across your face. The feeling of satisfaction is sharp and purely physical – a rapid firing of nerve endings in the brain stem. And as quickly vanishes. For you must now return to the edge of the wood where another seared carcass no doubt waits to be crushed, another grub no doubt waits to be seized. And you must pretend not to notice that, in the meantime, your child's wings have grown and thickened, web-wet, that his eyes have further eclipsed and now shoot out practice sparks, that he'll soon be ready to join the others in their intricate, never-ending devastation.

You must pretend not to notice.

# THE LIFE AND TIMES OF HARRY QUICK, P.I.

## I

### Past tense; future even more tense.

It's at moments like this, in the middle of the damned night, a rusty rain falling, dripping off my fedora and soaking my shoulders, that I say to myself: Harry Quick, why oh why didn't you listen to the folks that made you instead of being as stubborn as a bloody mule – and almost as extinct? There you were, a most promising young lad, ready to take the world by storm, gulping down population calculus and combinatory history almost as quickly as they were being invented – and what happened? The girls thought you were the swellest. They said you knew how to treat them right. The profs liked you. They said you were someone with a head on his shoulders. And everybody but everybody said you would go places.

Oh, I went places all right. Like this place, for instance, where I'm pushed up hard against a damp thorny wall in the middle of the night with infrared camera in hand waiting for someone who might or might not come and knowing I'll spend quite a few more nights doing this over and over (till you get it right, Harry Quick, and then some).

How can I be so sure, you ask? Well, for that I'd have to tell you the whole sordid tale, wouldn't I? And you know what that means, eh? The old throat gets dry PDQ. A drink? Sure, why not? Can't do me any harm, can it? I guarantee it's a tale that'll hold your attention, even if – Ssh! There's someone coming! This might be it! How the hell do you work this contraption? Oh yeah. That's right. There – got them in my sights. Damn! Another false alarm. Just a young couple looking for a dry spot. Say, about that drink... and as long as you're paying...

Ah, that's better. Anyway, it all starts. Or started – don't mind me if I get my tenses all mixed up, I was never that good at them – on a morning much like any other. The lights that kept the city bright the night long slowly dimmed and a much-filtered, much-improved sun took their place.

"Wake up, Harry," a sultry, creamy voice whispered, the voice of my fondest dreams, wet and otherwise. "Rise and shine, lover boy."

When I simply turned over and tried to resume snoring, the voice changed its tone:

"Harry. I see it's just as hard for you to get up in the morning as it is at night."

"Shut up, will ya!"

"Come on, you wimp-assed excuse for a cum stain, get to work. We can't live on snores and farts. Your clients—"

I suddenly sat bolt upright in my bed and hurled the pillow across the room.

"Bullseye," I said, rubbing my hands together.

"Okay, Harry," the voice said, getting weaker, "if that's the way you want it. But don't blame me if you never get nowhere. Don't blame me..."

And it petered out completely. And to think some people actually had an amanuensis that walked around and couldn't be shut off. I'd go bananas.

No matter what, though, there was no way I could go back to sleep. So I threw the covers off and stepped out of bed. The room began its morning ritual of going from sleeping quarters to office. The bed receded into the wall ("Didn't make it again, eh Harry?"); a tacky desk took its place; the lighting changed from romantic shadow effect to fluorescent direct; several wall panels slid back to reveal the outside world (of which this 20th-storey flat was part and parcel); finally, the floor opened up and a tri-v popped into view.

"Coffee," I said. "Where's the coffee?"

There was no answer.

"All right," I said. "I apologize for throwing the pillow. Now, where's my coffee?"

"Sorry, sir," the voice said icily. "Coffee allowance used up for the week."

"This is ridiculous. It's only Tuesday. And I gotta have my java."

"You had six and a quarter cups yesterday, sir. The day before, eight cups. The day before that—"

"All right, all right. Spare me."

I reached into my desk drawer and pulled out a bottle of the smoothest. I took a swig, then stuck a hard-edged toothbrush in my mouth and flicked on the tri-v. Ah, a P.I.'s life is a grand life, I told myself. No suit and tie; no punch clock; no rat race; no stupid bosses looking over your shoulder. I yawned and leaned back on the pillow which I'd managed to retrieve. Not much business lately – and that's the way I liked it. So, some people called me picky because I wouldn't take run-of-the-millers like sniffing out rich runaways or shit like that. But I left that to the electronic watchdogs who could be tuned to the frequency of everyone in the city.

On the tube, a holographic horror who passed herself off as a latter-day fundamentalist (you could tell by the waist-length beard and braided armpits) was giving her version of the ongoing robot-human controversy.

"Yea verily," she said, gesticulating frantically. "Till now the robots have realized who were the masters and who the servants. God created the robots to serve mankind, to go forth to the airless places and do mankind's bidding. Now, rumours are reaching Metro of unhappiness and rebellions among those servants on some of the Outer Colonies."

"Where ya been, lady," I said. "Some of them rumours are 50 years old."

"Is it possible," she said, slitting her eyes the way she did whenever she was about to ask a pointed rhetorical question, "that our safeguards weaken in direct proportion to the distance from the source of creation? If that is so... mark my words... if that is so, then we shall never be safe. For we are the creatures of natural selection and our weakness is bound together with our strength. Remember, we evolved from slime and to slime will return."

"Speak for yourself, scumbag!" I shouted and jabbed at the remote control.

I kept jabbing and twisting till I came to the morning news. No, I'm not talking about the regular news. This is a series of flashing headlines for the benefit of those who can still read. When the cursor's on the headline, you can ask for more details – or move on to the next. I preferred that to a grinning pretty-person telling me 10 million died when Uranus let off a bit of gas and burned away half of the Miranda colony. Anyway, the main headline for the morning was the repairing of a stubborn tear in the outer shell of some space station or other. But the item that caught my attention was tucked away just above the revised freighter charges for sub-space shipment to Ganymede.

TWO ROBOTS FOUND DEACTIVATED, the headline read. I positioned the cursor and pressed *Enter* on the remote: "Last evening, two robots from the park cleaning brigade were discovered completely inoperative. All efforts to revive them proved futile. An examination showed that their electronic circuits had been fused. Witnesses claim to have seen a mysteriously dressed person leaving the scene just prior to the finding of the robots."

What the hell, I thought. Must be some nut who objects to sharing the street with a coupla bolt-heads. Or maybe he's been listening to that fundamentalist bullshit. Two days later, another robot – a trendy new model destined to control the comp link-up with Mars – was found in exactly the same condition. To show that he had no preferences, this madman next picked on a poor, old obsolete guy who'd outlived any possible purpose and was peacefully rusting away on a park bench. The sot was still clutching his cheap mechanic's oil when they found him. Maybe, he was lucky at that. That oil would've frizzled his brain almost as quickly as the laser did.

Well, let me tell you. The news didn't stay just above the revised Ganymede shipping rates for long. By week's end, every grinning pretty-person had it top item with stock shots of robots ("a robot just like this one..."), talking-head experts and dire warnings.

It was the beginning of a Metro-wide panic. Robots no longer dared walk the streets at night unless they were in groups

– "gangs" the fundamentalists called 'em. There was some talk of going about armed but that's all it was – so far. Everyone knows robots can't kill. It just isn't in their nature.

Some humans, the more insensitive ones, wondered out loud what all the fuss was about. After all, robots weren't like humans. They didn't really die. So their brains fused. Big deal. All you had to do was replace their old ones with new ones. Of course, they wouldn't be quite the same as before, experience being what it is as a shaper of personality. But that was nothing compared to complete extinction, compared to the reduction to nullity a human undergoes. Or is supposed to undergo. No one knows for sure, do they?

The very same morning they found the derelict, I got a call from Captain R.X. Layton – Rex to his friends but Ex-Lax to most, head of the Robot Control Division for Metro Security. I had worked for him before running afoul of some bureaucrat's well-placed procedural booby trap.

"Harry, how's it going?" he asked, making sure his back was to me so I couldn't see him on the vidphone. "Business treating you all right?"

"Splendid, Captain. And busy as all outdoors. Now, what the hell do you want?"

"Rex. Call me, Rex. Been watching the news?"

"Only the sports and nothing but. I'm a fanatic for 50-man weightless Betelgeusian pedal-ball. But you still haven't answered my question, Rex."

I knew what was coming but I wasn't about to say. I wanted to hear it from him.

"Harry," he said, swivelling in his chair so I could see his oh-so-concerned face, "we've got trouble. Big trouble. You can't begin to imagine the trouble we've got."

That's when I should've hung up, slammed the phone down and gone back to waiting for that rich shock-head to walk in wearing nothing but a full-length stim synth-fur which she'd proceed to shed and spread on the floor and...

Instead, I took a drink and let old Ex-Lax continue: "We need some fresh ideas on this. The guy's got us stumped."

"What's the problem... Rex? The entire Metro security force can't find one little old madman with a primitive laser beam? Is that it, Rex?"

He jumped up. "How the hell do you know about that?" he bellowed. "Nobody's supposed—"

"Sit down, Rex, before you rupture yourself. I didn't know what the weapon was until you leaped up and told me."

He sat down again. "We just can't seem to get a handle on it. Lots of eyewitnesses. Eyewitnesses coming out of the wazoo. Like he doesn't make any effort to hide himself or nothing. But the bastard always vanishes before we can put the squeeze on him. I don't mind telling you we're desperate."

"Is that so, Rex? Gee, I wouldn't have known."

"Look, Harry, will you... will you..."

"Help. Is that the word stuck in your gullet?"

"Yes, dammit. We need he... hel..."

"Well, I don't know, Rex. I'm right in the middle of a rich shock-head case. And you know how those ladies are? They want your undivided attention."

"All kidding aside, Harry. If we don't put the grab on this loonie – and fast, there's no telling what might happen. Retaliation, riots, war even. And, if it comes to war—"

"We'll win, Rex. There's no doubt about it."

"Harry, you know as well as I do it's a no-win situation. Everything we've built up – the co-existence of human and robot to create the greatest society this world's ever seen – will come tumbling down. Do you want that? Already, there's talk among the robotics crowd to disconnect some of the categorical imperatives. At least so the robots can fire back in self-defence. Once that starts…"

"All right, all right." I took a drink. Ugh! Always hated the stuff. Goes right through me. "You've convinced me. But I don't work as a philanthropist, you know."

"Harry," he said in that oily way he has when he knows he's got you hooked, "you solve this and your future's set."

My future? Give it back, please. At the time, all I could think was: Sonuvabitch! Why do I always allow myself to get suckered in? Why? Because of that huge ego of yours, Harry, old buddy. Because there ain't no crime you can't solve, right. Because everything you own is really on loan and the reward from this could get you a vacation on Paradise Colony and maybe even a bigger coffee allowance – now wouldn't that be something? But mainly because you're an idiot, Harry. An idiot with lots and lots of time on his hands.

## II
### Just stand still – and trust me, Squiggy.

Did I really think I could do it when the entire Metro police department had failed? Who knows what I thought. All I know is that it wasn't hard to convince Squiggy, my faithful pal and partner, to lend a hand. Of course, it hasn't been hard ever since… well, ever since I rewired his circuits into believing I had saved his life from the dreaded triple-M Mongol Marsupial Monster – whatever that may be.

"Are you sure it's safe, Harry?" the big lovable hunk asked as he clanged along beside me.

"Of course, it's safe. Would I lie to you?" He shook his head and I made sure he couldn't see my ugly prevaricating face. "All you have to do is sit on the park bench looking like a derelict. That's not hard, now is it?"

"But Harry, I saw…"

"Since when have you been wasting so much time watching the tri-v and since when do you believe that shit?" He looked down. Get him now, quick, Quick. "Well, then, what's the problem?" He shrugged his shoulders. I had him now. "Trust me, Squiggy," I said, putting an arm around him and squeezing – well, metaphorically speaking anyway. "That poor excuse for Mongol Marsupial Monster spit won't even get the chance to lift his pinky before I zap him right between the eyes."

Well, it almost turned out that way and that "almost" still brings shivers when I think about it. The stake-out took place in a park. We waited for Metro Security to dim the lights locally and turn off the sidewalks and I hid myself behind what passes these days for bushes – God help the cow that takes a bite. It wasn't a whole lot of fun, especially when some wise guy decided to increase the chill factor and lay out a bit of mist. Artistes, sheesh. But I'm used to night work and the damp just made these creaky old joints move a little more slowly, that's all.

Squiggy was another matter entirely. He squirmed on the bench like someone being put through an ionized free-radical test. When he could sit no more, he'd suddenly leap up and pace. I swear if it had been real grass, he would have worn a hole six feet deep. He looked around nervously from side to side. There was no one else on the streets. The authorities had arranged it so that everyone stayed inside so we could increase our chances of catching the guy. All Squiggy had for company was a stupid little squirrel that the city had forgotten to service and that probably thought of Squiggy as its mate from the way it kept offering him nuts. After about the tenth time, Squiggy kicked it away so that it fell over on its side. And there the poor thing lay, trying desperately to right itself but succeeding only in going in circles.

It was even harder to convince Squiggy to try it again the following night. In the end, I had to sweeten the pot with the promise of a libation (another small rearrangement of his circuits).

"All right," he said, taking a healthy swig of the finest 20W50. "But this is it. No more."

We tried another part of the park, near a grove of mock maple trees and close to the spot where the maniac had struck once before. Squiggy sat huddled on the bench mumbling to himself. It was getting on to morning and I was just thinking I'd have to come up with another promise I couldn't keep when a figure emerged out of the shadows. He was dressed like nothing I'd ever since before. Or maybe I had – but only in a museum. He stood there for a moment, eyes and face shaded by a dark, broad-brimmed hat, body wrapped in some sort of black cape, trimmed in outlandish purple velvet. I tensed, ready to strike at the bastard's first false move.

I never got the chance. In one motion, the man threw open his cape, held out his arm and fired a beam in the direction of my friend.

"Squiggy!" I shouted, hurling myself toward the madman.

It was too late. The beam hit Squiggy square on the forehead and then bounced off to dissipate in the night sky. Oh Buddha, I thought. Squiggy jerked up straight as a twanging arrow, reeled backwards a few steps, stumbled a bit and then collapsed onto the patent-pending grass.

"I'm done," he said in a pathetic voice. "It's the end for me."

I hesitated for a moment before giving chase. The man had turned and was striding quickly through the park. But he didn't seem to be making any effort to hide. I thought, Boy, this guy's a real loonie. How could the cops have missed him? I shouted for him to stop, visions of Paradise Colony dancing before me. To my surprise, he did stop. And turned. That's when I decided I'd better pull up as well. We were about 20 metres apart. Right behind him was the mock maple grove.

"You'd better give yourself up," I said, trying to keep the falsetto out of my voice. "The Metro Security Forces have this park surrounded. The sidewalks are switched off. There's no way out of here."

As if right on cue, the sirens started to blare and the park was flooded with lights. From every direction, helmeted police wearing electromagnetic shields converged on the robot-killer. But he just stood there.

"Come out," I said, taking a step forward. "The situation's hopeless for you."

Keep talking to him, I told myself. That way he won't think of using that gizmo in his hand.

"Throw your weapon down now and give yourself up. We can help you. There's nothing to be afraid of." Nothing at all. We'll just rework a few of *your* brain cells, that's all.

I thought he was actually going to turn himself in when he lifted his hand as if to wave, calmly looked at his watch and stepped behind one of the maple trees.

"We've got him," I yelled. "We've got him. The Robot-Killer Mystery has been solved."

Sure it had. Except that when we closed in, there was nothing behind the tree. He was gone, vanished, zippo squat. We looked like a ripe bunch of bananas, flashing our lights on that poor tree and ordering it to drop its weapons. The police, after making sure there was no other way out, scoured the park centimetre by centimetre, using the electronic sniffers for good measure. Nada. He couldn't have escaped – but he had.

I went back to the bench and sat on it, making like The Thinker himself. Squiggy was lying on the ground where he'd so melodramatically fallen.

"Okay, you old coward. You can get up now. He's gone."

He activated one eye, then the other. "You mean you didn't catch him?"

"Afraid not."

"Harry," he said, standing up, "I'm not doing this again. No-sirree, Bob. Not for all the mechanic's oil in Metro. If I could've crapped my pants, I would've."

"All right, don't make such a big deal. Have another swig."

I took a half-filled mickey out of my pocket and handed it to him. He grabbed it with two shaking hands and gulped down the contents, spilling a goodly portion over himself.

"Jeez," I said. "You all right?"

"Oh sure, sure. I'm just peachy keen. Some maniac nearly splatters the few brains I've got left across a park, that's all. Nothing serious."

"Good. Glad to hear it. Now, let's go home and think this thing through."

So why wasn't he fried, you ask? That's a secret best kept between me and the mirror with the diffusion prism I'd taped to his head. Pretty ingenious, huh? And original, too. I told Squiggy it was an old, tried-and-tested trick of mine but only so he wouldn't worry unnecessarily. Besides, if it hadn't worked Squiggy would never have known.

## III
### "Hmm, this calls for a bit of thought."

"Teleportation is out of the question," Professor Caraway was saying – or at least that's what came out of his left head. "You can't be teleported without the proper machinery. Besides, the energy required would set off every electronic watchdog in the Quadrant."

I sat across from him in his cozy, cluttered office at the university. Out of the plate glass window, I could see a group of students demonstrating, marching back and forth. There was plenty of shouting and banners that read Robots Defend Yourselves and Down With Fat, Lazy Capitalist Humans. I was glad to see things hadn't changed much since I'd been there – except then it had been the humans protesting.

"Harry, are you listening?"

"Huh! I'm sorry, Professor. No, he couldn't have teleported himself. No machinery in the park and no unusual energy peaks."

"Hmmm. This calls for a bit of thought."

When Professor Aristotle Augustine Aquinas Caraway's twin crania called for a bit of thought, you had better be ready to sit out the night. Head of the n-dimensional math department and holistic history at Metro U, the professor had his hand in just about everything that went on in the city. This kept him pretty occupied since he had only one appendage that could be loosely called a hand – right in the middle of his plexi-form chest. In fact, nothing could disconcert a student more quickly than to see that snaking out toward him.

Caraway was the university's pride and joy, the most brilliant thinking machine – and therefore thinker – they had. There was nothing monstrous or arbitrary about his two heads. They served the same purpose as the split brain in human beings. While his left head concentrated on verbalizing and thinking things through, the right concerned itself with patterns and intuitions. He had been created as an experiment – the first robot to be not only logical but also with the ability to go beyond logic. Officially, it had been a failure, but the truth was nobody wanted more than one Caraway around – and that included Caraway himself.

I first met Triple A, as we called him behind his back, when I was an eager young buck at Metro U. There we were, the cream of the educational crop, fresh from our training schools and anxious to prove we belonged. We were ready to take the world by the tail and heave it out to another galaxy. We were superior, unlike the lazy ones who wanted nothing but to be served and who could no longer even read or write, let alone accept responsibility. We were as cocky as comets. Until he floated into the class, that is.

From the moment I saw him, his two heads swivelling, his appendage snaking, I knew I'd better bone up on my n-dimensional math – and damn quick. I boned up all the way to the top of the class. By year's end, we had become what could best be described as friends. Ironically, it was Professor Caraway who advised me not to waste my time with math.

"Mathematicians are a dime a dozen," he said. "All it takes is a special type of programming. I could turn my grandmother into one – if I had a granny. What you've got, my boy, is a certain intuitive characteristic all but lacking today. I guess it can best be called the ability to do the right thing at the right time without really knowing why."

When I asked what profession I might be fit for, he said only that I would find out in time. In time? Was that a little joke of his?

The demonstration outside threatened to turn violent. Several human passersby had started shouting back at the protestors and, when ignored, they picked up pieces of earth to hurl at them. The campus police were called in, but it wasn't really necessary since clods of earth couldn't possibly hurt the robots and they'd never retaliate in any event. Would they?

Professor Caraway purred contentedly and both his heads lit up. He wheeled rapidly back and forth across the office, occasionally plugging himself into a computer terminal. That meant only one thing. He had an idea. But I knew enough to wait for him to calm down before asking him about it. When in the grip of an intuition, his right head takes over – and naturally all he can do is sputter and whir. If you ask him anything, he'll just wave his arm up and down – and it can get mighty dangerous, a bit like being caught in a food processor. Finally, after a few more minutes, he stopped pacing. Identically spectrummed beams of beatific smiles spread slowly across his faces.

"Harry, Harry, Harry," he said, coiling his arm around me and squeezing ever so gently. "Harry, I don't know what it is, nor do I ever hope to understand, but your presence inspires me. You can't imagine how many times I've sat here stumped, depressed, unable to solve a problem. And then you called or paid me a visit and there it was – the answer. It had been there all—"

"Professor!"

"Yes, what is it?"

Good lord agnostic of the universe! What an act! Professor Caraway was not in the least absent-minded. Like all robots, he had perfect retention. Problem is he's seen too many tri-v *Absent-minded Perfesser* holos.

"Oh yes," he said. "The Case of the Missing Robot Killer. It's simple. The mistake you and our very able constabulary have been making is in assuming the killer is actually there at the scene of the crime."

"What! Professor, have your wires gone a bit haywire? Of course we assume his presence at the scene of the crime. How else could you explain his presence – at the scene of the crime?"

"By projection, of course."

By projection, of course! That would explain both his sudden appearances and even more sudden disappearances. He wasn't really there. Only a projection of himself. Only a tri-d image of directed light. And that would explain his weapon as well. But wait a minute. I was getting a bit ahead of myself. That didn't explain how he did it at all. We didn't possess the technology to direct a person's projection in any physical sense so that he could act on material objects. Holographic images, yes, but that was the extent of it.

"You're absolutely right," the professor said.

I felt like sticking a finger between my lips and reciting all the trigono-historic formulae I'd ever been taught.

"Nevertheless," Caraway said, noting my consternation, "that doesn't make it impossible. Not at all impossible."

He turned and stared out the window.

"You know, Harry," he said sadly, "we're witnessing the end of one very enjoyable world. Not to say it wouldn't have happened anyway, but these killings have certainly speeded things up. Those robots out there are angry. And frustrated. The only thing that prevents them from taking up arms right now and defending themselves is that robots, unlike most humans, are moral beings with well-defined standards of right and wrong. What's been happening has muddled their thinking processes. I'm afraid, Harry. I'm afraid they'll soon start thinking like humans."


## IV
### Rumblings, disaster, and damage control.

During the next few weeks, consternation turned to panic. No more robot killings were reported but it seemed the damage had already been done. Influential robots in government and industry started to press for stricter controls over humans, some even going so far as to demand a curfew between lights-on and sunrise. Humans retaliated by roaming about at night in packs, singing and shouting inflammatory and insulting statements as they linked arms and rode down dusky streets. Skirmishes became more frequent and each led to an automatic reprogramming of robot standards. An extremist group, Robots for Right Reason Society, called for the immediate implementation of self-defence circuits. It was much like the old descriptions of grasshoppers gathering to become locusts. Disaster was definitely in the air. You couldn't turn on the tri-v without seeing the holograph of some important robot or human pointing, jabbing wildly and screaming at the top of his/her lungs.

"My fellow robots/humans. We have come to that point in our history where coexistence is no longer possible. Nor perhaps even desirable. We have lived in equilibrium now for close to a generation, ever since the great/infamous first robot thought for himself without the help of an incompetent/indispensable human. Who's at fault for tilting the balance? We all know. What can we do about it? We all know that as well, don't we?"

The saner, more level-headed among us were grateful civilians no longer carried weapons. But crude ones could always be made – pieces of flint, hammers, parts of appliances, etc. And it's funny how the most inane object can turn dangerous. It had not come to that... yet. However, the most ominous rumblings came from the Internal Security Forces. Hints of discontent till now, subtle questioning of authority. After all, why should a robot take orders from a human commander and vice versa?

"One more robot killing and we'll have out-and-out civil war," I said, sitting pensively on my favourite stool at the Come-By-Chance bar.

Squiggy nodded – and almost fell off his chair. A man and woman danced sensuously, so close you couldn't tell where one started and the other ended. In a dim corner another robot sat with his back to the wall, scanning the room with his photoelectric cells.

"Funny," I said, taking another sip from a bubbling concoction in front of me and grimacing at its taste, "but I'm almost relieved it's happening. Naw, I don't mean that. Maybe it's my childhood. Do you know I was found in a field with no idea how I got there?"

"Sure, sure, bosh," Squiggy said, slurring his words badly. He could no longer focus – and that was making me dizzy.

"You've had too much, you old sot. Why don't you let the sidewalk take you around the block so you can burn it off? Go on, now. We'll need our wits about us in the morning."

"Shay, bosh, you're absho... absho... absholootly right." He stood up and tottered from side to side. "We've got to... to have our... r... r bits... our fits... "

He wove out of the bar and into the street like he'd done a hundred times before. I turned and ordered another drink – just to wash the first one down, of course. There was a tap on my shoulder – and the smell of perfume (I won't say what kind). It was the woman who had been sensuous dancing.

"Say, honey," she purred. "How about one for me, too? That creep left me with nothing but my self-respect."

I've never been one to say *nyet* to a lady – or a reasonable facsimile thereof – especially if she's observant enough to praise my muscles of steel.

I was relaxing in my bedroom-office the following morning, trading banter with my disembodied voice of conscience ("She wasn't bad, Harry, but you're definitely slipping") when the call came in from Captain Layton.

"Say Rex, finally come up with a prescription that'll help us solve these murders? Or is this a social call?"

He frowned and looked down at a sheet of paper in front of him.

"Come on, now," I said, sipping slowly on my last cuppa for the week – and it was only Monday. "Don't tell me it's so serious you've lost that famous sense of humour?"

"Harry, there's been another robot killing."

I leapt up from my chair. "What! When? Where? How come I didn't see it on the news? Forget that last question."

"Harry, I think you'd better come down here."

⚜

When I walked out of the bowels of the Metro Security Building, I was filled with an emotion I'd never experienced before –

pure, unadulterated hate. The filthy, skulking, cowardly Venusian flypaper rat had killed my best friend. He'd waited in ambush for a poor, drunken robot who'd never harmed anyone in his whole life.

The police had found Squiggy early that morning crumpled over near a pile of garbage, his circuits fused into one solid mass, one lump of silicon and platinum. And pinned to him like you would a sack of potatoes, the killer had left a note: "Naughty boy. You fooled me the other night. A good trick that mirror, but I've got plenty of time. Robots are a menace. They start off cuddly and cute but if we don't destroy them now, they'll take over the world. I know that even if you poor sorry creatures don't seem to. Until we meet again."

Until we meet again. Yes, you're goddamn right we'll meet again, I vowed. Squiggy wasn't just a scrap heap of metal to me, not something put together to simulate thinking and feeling. He'd saved my life so many times I'd lost count. He was kind and gentle and more human than most humans. The closest I've ever come to tears was when they threw back that sheet down at the recycling centre and his empty beamers stared back at me. I'll get him for you, Squiggy. He's made a mistake this time. I'll get him if it's the last thing I do.

I got so plastered that night – on real drinks, too – that Four-Armed Al the bartender volunteered to drive me home. Halfway there, I changed my mind and told him to take me to the university instead. I had a theory I wanted to try out on Professor Caraway. It wasn't original actually. Just an extension of his.

When I finally got home, I noticed a light on in my office. No, I told myself. He wouldn't have the nerve to do that. Besides, the code would only work with my voice. I threw the door open and stepped back.

"Squiggy!" I shouted before I was able to control myself.

"I beg your pardon, sir," the gleaming, spanking-new robot said. "I am SQ-2 at your service."

He looked like Squiggy and he walked like Squiggy, but he certainly didn't sound like Squiggy. I walked in and sat down, opening the drawer.

"How's about a nightcap?" I said, holding up the bottle of Grade A.

"Sorry, sir. I don't partake."

Well, I said to myself, looks like there's a few more wires to rearrange around here.

## V

### Just in time – and time and time again.

I was sure the robot killer would accept my challenge. After all, why would he bother with a note if he wasn't looking for a fight? So I used the tri-v to broadcast one in return. No matter where he was, he obviously knew what went on and must be monitoring us in some way. Once again Squiggy would serve as the decoy. It was easier this time because he didn't know he'd been through it before. But I still had to keep reassuring him there was nothing to be afraid of.

"Don't worry, Squiggy, old boy," I said, making sure not to look him in the eye.

"All you have to do is stand around looking like some bored tourist from Aldebaran, or an awestruck hick from some god-forsaken asteroid. I'll be right there, hidden from view but ready to blast that fiend back to whatever hellhole he's spawned from."

It was beautiful on the 200th floor of the Jupiter Building. In fact, there's no more breathtaking sight in the entire Metro area. The sky was criss-crossed with beams of light, each a different colour and each coded for the essential service it performed. There was even a broadband for weather control. That high above the earth it was also possible to make out the thousands of satellites that circled the planet. And if one had good enough eyes one might even be able to see the original site of our first space colony, an eerie display of green fluorescing in the deep sky.

It was nothing but a natural museum now where the curious were taken on guided tours and honeymooners spent their precious moments together. "Isn't it strange how we get used to things and miss the newness in them," I whispered to Professor Caraway, huddled with me in the doorway to the elevator that could whisk us down to the ground floor in the blinking of an eye. I'd agreed to Caraway's presence at the last moment in case he could spot something that would help pin our killer down.

Squiggy was out in the open, leaning on the force-field that prevented people from falling those 200 floors. It gave way slightly with his weight and then settled back to support him in a cocoon of magnetic energy. Squiggy dipped into his pocket and pulled out a bottle. Well, that's a little more like the old Squiggy, I thought. Now if I could only wean him away from calling me "Sir."

"I guess he's not as stupid as I thought," I whispered after we'd waited for several hours and even the natural beauty of the surroundings had worn off. "He doesn't seem to have taken the bait."

The words were hardly out of my mouth when a halo of light materialized between us and Squiggy. The light hesitated a moment and then became a distinct human figure in broad-rimmed hat and black cape.

"I was right!" Caraway exclaimed with both heads at once. "It is a projection!"

Caraway lit up so badly he couldn't get another word out. Squiggy backed away toward the far end of the building. I alone stood there pretending I did this sort of thing every second day. I'd better be right, I kept telling myself. Otherwise, the whole world's going up.

"Well, well," I said as casually as possible. "If it isn't our maniac robot killer in his fancy-ball get up."

"Mr. Quick. That's your name, isn't it?"

I nodded and took a step toward him. Get as close as possible, Quick.

"Mr. Quick, you are an intelligent and decent man, but you're fighting for the wrong side. After all, what are a bunch of godless metallic heaps to you?"

Godless? I was right! "I don't like to see innocent people get hurt."

"Innocent people!" he exclaimed. "These aren't innocent people. These are the destroyers of our beautiful world. These are the vile creations of man, the tools that will finally eliminate him and take over his rightful place in the world. I'm here to see that it doesn't happen. And I'll destroy anyone who gets in my way."

Professor Caraway made a squawking noise and hid behind me.

"But that won't really be necessary, will it?" he said, smiling. "Already, with just a few zappings I've started your society on its spiral toward oblivion."

"Isn't it your society as well?" I looked up to see one of Captain Layton's men hovering over the killer's head, holding an electro-lasso of the type used to immobilize troublemakers. No! I said to myself. Get out of here. You'll scare him away. I tried to motion with my hand for the policeman to get out of there. No use. Keep the killer occupied or he'll look up. "What kind of society do you expect to get out of the ashes of this one?"

"One totally without tools, without machines, without—"

"No!" I shouted. "You idiots!"

But it was too late. The Security policeman spun out the lasso and dropped it over the black-clad figure. He froze beneath the force field.

"We've got him!" the policeman and Squiggy yelled at the same time.

"I'm afraid not," Caraway said. "What you have there is just an image, an image composed of some sort of charged ion field."

"Correct, Professor," he said. "And now farewell."

He held up his weapon and was just about to blast Professor Caraway when I made my jump. The moment I hit him we began to dematerialize and the last thing I heard was Caraway's voice: "He's done it! The young fool has done it!"

So what had I done? Oh, nothing at all. I just got myself stranded, that's all. There I was whirling through space, hanging on for dear life, thinking all the while, I've got him now. Wherever he goes, I go. He can't escape me. And then I'll drag him back to Metro to face the music.

It was a good plan, a very good plan. Except for one thing. I wasn't whirling in space. Goodbye, Caraway. So long, Squiggy. I'll see you sometime. Maybe.

When the spinning stopped, I found myself seated on top of the robot killer right in the middle of a large laboratory. It was so primitive he still used actual beakers and test tubes instead of magma-containers. Something else out of the museum.

"Get off me!" he screamed, now very much flesh and blood. "The apparatus wasn't made for two. Get off before it explodes. You'll kill us both, you fool!"

I certainly didn't want that to happen, so I hurled myself away from him, scrambling to get out of the way. Overhead, the apparatus, a dome-shaped contraption fed by a plethora of multi-coloured wires, glowed menacingly in the dark. As I dashed out the door, the killer reached up and started frantically throwing switches. Too late. The apparatus suddenly imploded and the entire room became a sharp flash of light, so bright I was forced to cover my eyes for a moment. There was a horrible scream.

When I opened my eyes again, I thought I saw him silhouetted against the sky. Then the room vanished and him with it – now nothing perhaps but a pile of molecules scattered across the vortices of time and space. Why, maybe some of them even fell back on the world I'd been so abruptly forced to leave behind.

## VI
### Time, Gentlemen. Please.

During the next few days, I thought long and hard about that world. Would it survive now that it was safe from the robot killer? Or had the damage already been done? Was it even the same world? Ah, what was the use of asking such questions? It was obvious I'd never know the answers to them. Here I was, in pre-robotic days, surrounded by nothing but humans. Oh, they had some primitive thinking machines but none advanced enough for companionship, let alone drinking partners.

And it rained here – uncontrolled rain. That's right. I first saw it the night after the implosion. The killer's house, still standing except for the one room that had been sheered off cleanly, was situated in a dense wood – a real forest! – outside the city proper. Dressed in my host's clothes, I started to walk toward the lights that from afar resembled those of Metro.

The resemblance faded quickly. For one thing, the ground was muddy and pockmarked with puddles and you could stand there on the sidewalk all night and not get anywhere because it damned well wasn't about to move. For another, the buildings on the edge of the city were in the process of crumbling. Some had already been demolished while others leaned precariously, teetering on the very verge of destruction. And yet I saw shadows in the doorways, men and women dressed in rags, drinking from paper bags, falling over into the puddles, blubbering, urinating, fighting, trying to have sex. I shuddered and moved on, still nourishing the hope that there was a way to get back, that neither time nor anything else is a one-way slope.

Why, in fact, wasn't that a familiar field, a childhood playground? And, look, there must be libraries around. Not full of tapes and spools and holographic images perhaps, but at least books. Thank God, I'd taken the time to learn how to read. And, surely, amid all those books there would be some mention of a time projection machine. Hopefully then I might be able to return if not materially at least as an image. And then there was no telling how quickly Professor Caraway would figure it all out.

Using the killer's name, I became a member of the city's central library. It had thousands upon thousands of books. I quickly scanned them all. Nowhere could I find such a device, except in speculative fiction books – and none of those explained how to create one. I searched the other libraries with the same result. Nor could anyone at the university help me. Where was Professor Caraway when I needed him?

I had been several months in that place becoming more and more depressed. I wandered through the primitive city in a complete daze, bumping into other pedestrians and walking across highways – jammed with vehicles rushing about helter-skelter – without even bothering to look where I was going. I, too, spent my time in doorways, thinking about the future. And I could feel my mind slowly closing on me, slowly shutting more and more doors. But I couldn't let the last one clang shut.

That's when, little by little, the old spirit returned. I wasn't a quitter, no sir. I wasn't a loser. Hadn't I been Caraway's best student? Hadn't I solved a crime that might have destroyed us all? Wasn't I a topnotch P.I.? Damned right, I was. Even here in the midst of a most alien civilization – and I use the term loosely – I would adapt. I would adapt to muggings and unmoving sidewalks and even to having only humans for friends.

Didn't I come from the future? Didn't I already know the future existed while these poor souls would struggle to find out, would learn only through bloody trial and error? Why should I sit around moping when there was a world out there screaming to be fed, demanding to be solved?

## VII
### A job is a job – gotta get back.

And that's how I landed this job. Well, a P.I.'s life isn't all glamour and rich shock-heads, you know. There's plenty of standing against dirty, thorny walls, off the edge of overgrown parks filled with disgustingly real trees and the drip drip of acid rain. But it has its rewards, you know. Like what? Well, it really builds up character, you know. And knowing you've helped makes you feel all warm inside.

What's that? Would I do it again? Damned right, I would. And will when the time comes.

Thanks for the drink, pal. Sorry I can't finish it. But that's okay. I got a mickey of Grade A right here in my pocket. Gotta get back.

# THE LIZARD AND THE LADY

While no one dares go so far as to openly deny their love for each other, it is no secret that the marriage of the Lizard creature (be it ever so upstanding on two hind legs) and the Earthwoman is one mainly of convenience. Especially now that her pregnancy has been announced. Or so goes the tongue-wagging, unable to wrap itself around the idea of two so different actually being happy together, let alone in love.

After many years of fruitless discussions, attempts at compromise and even the creation of mutual games, war threatened the two planets – one still to be born and the other mired in the past. It was decided that the next-best thing to all-out war would be a strategic marriage.

When the leader of the Lizard Transtemporal Expeditionary Force thought up the idea, with the aid of Pope John XXII, he knew better than to claim credit for it. Instead, he allowed the diplomatic pouch containing it to come into the hands of high-ranking Earth officials who then proposed the idea to him. He accepted with reluctance, his last bit of diplomatic business before being recalled for allowing the pouch to fall into Earth's hands.

The marriage took place between his son and the daughter of the Terrestrial Extra-Territorial Diplomatic Potentate to his planet. She volunteered because she felt she, better than any other woman on Earth, understood lizards, not only having spent several years in their midst but also having raised several as a child. (Of course, she told no one she dissected them when they died, although she might then have been able to claim she knew them inside out.) Besides, she could never turn down an adventure.

They have set up housekeeping on a space station halfway in time between the two planets. The Lizard quickly settles into the pattern of social life offered and even adapts to the always-called-for smoking jacket. She makes the perfect wife, patient, understanding of his shortcomings (a tendency to dart his tongue out at nearby flies), beautiful, educated, calm, with a poise acquired through travel to the far corners of the universe. In private, they're polite and responsive to one another. In public, they're always seen arm-in-claw, smiling at each other and sending those who view them into fits of jealousy. And disbelief.

In one matter and one matter only does the diplomat's daughter refuse to compromise. This is in the question of sex. The Lizard tends to be cold-blooded and, if left alone, could go for months without a twitch. His pipe, his books, visual tapes, and intellectual conversations with philosophers from the past and future are more than enough. But she insists on – and receives – a sufficient dose to keep her contented, the details of which she describes in a diary hidden somewhere in the fifth century A.D. Vicious rumours (those that don't have this down as a marriage of convenience, of course) have it she lives for this alone. And it is true a gleam invades her eye when other women discuss the bedding abilities of their more mundane partners.

Meanwhile, higher-ups on both planets await the outcome of this marriage. On this rests all hope of peace in the future (in the future of the future). Doctors check her pregnancy daily. Theories are evolve as to whom the child will resemble. Will it begin as a lizard and become human or vice versa? Will it perhaps combine the qualities of both? Will it follow Mendel's Laws on short- and long-stemmed peas or Lizard Philopater's theories on regeneration? While the Lizards argue the ethics of such a child and humans compete in game shows trying to guess the exact date of its birth, name, weight, number of limbs, tongue length, skin colour, etc., peace reigns supreme over both planets.

# HOTHOUSE LOVE

*Gentle Mother, Dear Sisters and Brothers – may you continue to grow straight and tall, may your limbs remain supple, may the sweet Earth nourish and keep you healthy all the days of your lives. Above all, may you mercifully escape the fate awaiting our more unfortunate brethren in the years, centuries and eons to come – and, no matter what happens, may you have the strength and wisdom to go on giving thanks:*

Since it's my turn for storytelling and, since no one's permitted to shirk this duty – especially now that The Sleepers are on the verge of returning (hovering at this very moment like giant, black-winged angels in our pristine skies), I'd like to relate a tale from the dawn of time itself, one that I feel is more appropriate – and urgent – than ever. Yes, I'd like to tell the story of how Bob The Preacher and his good friend, the No-Name Puppy, saved a dying Earth from utter and total annihilation.

To begin with, his name wasn't Bob the Preacher in those days. Rather, if he called himself anything, it was Robert the Hobo. The "Hobo" in keeping with his lowly station in life: neither well-nourished nor well-rooted. And "Robert" because he truly disliked his childhood name of "Bob." It reminded him of bobbing for apples when such things were still in vogue. And

"Bob's your uncle." And bob-style haircuts. If someone had called him Bob before his preaching days, he would most likely not have responded – or responded in such a way as to let the person forcibly know how he felt about the name.

Needless to say, being a hobo with no place in which to retreat or take shelter, the winters proved to be extremely hard for Robert. Especially as he'd chosen one of the northern-most island cities as his home during a period when climate control wasn't what it is today. Many a time, he would roam along this city's icy shoreline (jogging and bicycle paths in more clement weather), a thin layer of fibreglass insulation stuffed in his coat as the only protection from the wind that came off the water with all the ferocity of a timber wolf. Timber wolf: *Canis lupus occidentalis* with glowing red eyes, drooling jaws, and a tendency to howl. Once extinct, only recently reconstructed and, perhaps, soon to be extinct again.

But, if the days were untenable, you can just imagine the nights. Or maybe you can't in the midst of your typically tropical Eden, spoilt sisters and brothers. When that hazy orange ball sank below the horizon, glittery on the iced fountain-sprays of water, the entire landscape would take on the appearance of a Plutonian moon – blistered and lethal for even the smallest patch of exposed flesh. And each night Robert prepared without wasted motion for the end, for that moment the sap inside him ran dry for the last time. He would slide down quietly against the nearest leeward wall and – head between his knees – fall into a deep sleep, half-expecting not to wake up in the morning. And then he could imagine himself staying in that position, like a slender weeping willow – or birch tree – broken-backed with snow, until the spring thaw brought warmth and renewed hope for the living and simple putrefaction for him.

It would have happened that way, too – if it hadn't been for "the miracle." Or rather the first in what is now a well-thumbed catalogue. Robert was crouched low against the side of a strange-looking structure that multiplied and reflected the setting sun in all its ghastliness and fare-thee-well splendour when he suddenly fell through one of the wall panels. Inside, it was palely dark, palely luminescent, with faint lights, it seemed, immense distances off. A blast of suffocatingly humid air took his breath away for a moment; he began to sweat beneath his layers of insulation; salty drops obscured his vision; and everything around him turned green and shimmery, as if he were seeing the world through a steamy shower curtain. But he didn't care if he were swimming in his own sweat, if every single cell in his body began to itch intolerably from the heat, if he were in danger of literally melting. He knew one thing and one thing only – he was warm, and the warmth was delicious. For the first time in weeks, he stuck his head out from where it had been jammed inside his collar to conserve heat. And he untwined his fingers. And he wiggled his toes.

"Replace the wall panel," a deep voice told him. "Or else the winter will follow you in like a highly unwelcomed guest."

Of course, that was Robert talking to himself, something he had been doing with great frequency in recent weeks as few of the people he met seemed interested in starting up a conversation – even after an act of kindness such as dropping a monetary unit of some kind into his outstretched palm. Not that Robert really minded, having always preferred his own company to that of others. Besides, what his own voice told him was normally good advice. So he pushed the panel back into its slot. Several of the screws were loose – a stroke of luck that explained why it had fallen in the first place. He retightened them enough for the panel to hold – but not so he couldn't make a quick getaway the moment someone unexpectedly rattled the front door. For he knew that, even in the wintertime, maintenance was needed to keep such a place going.

He wiped the perspiration from his eyes and, as he became accustomed to the dark, had his first good look around. There were plants everywhere – ferns and trees and vines of all kinds. He could hear fans high on the roof, blowing down hot air. Most of the plants had little lighted nameplates in front of them; a very few didn't. He realized then he was in a greenhouse – and that explained the reflection of the sun earlier in the evening. The higher portions of the building were made of large glass plates to capture as much daytime heat as possible. Why, look, from here Robert could even see the moon and a few of the stars – a miracle in itself in those days of perpetual smog.

Robert decided then and there to make the most of it. He didn't expect to stay in the greenhouse more than a night as the loose panel would definitely be spotted and fixed by the first worker to come in. But one night was more than he'd counted on. Like a reprieve, a temporary commutation of a sentence. So he took off his coat, the one stuffed with fibreglass insulation, and wrapped it into a serviceable pillow – along with his greasy toque and oversized mittens (the ones legend has it had been knitted by his invalid mother so many years before). Then, he removed his steel-toed boots and placed them to one side where he could reach them quickly – for fleeing or defence. Finally, he lay on his back and, taking the liberty of stretching (something he hadn't done since the temperature had dipped below zero), cartilage and ligaments snapping from disuse, he stared at the dark mass of leaves above him, their undulating and slightly glowing shadows lulling him gently but firmly to sleep.

It was, however, a strange kind of sleep – and filled with dreams that came in rapid succession, almost superimposed on one another. Of those he remembered the next morning, Robert couldn't quite decide if they were idyllic or nightmarish, full of hope or weighed down with foreboding. He dreamt, at one point, of a jungle – which he found only natural in a greenhouse setting. But this was a jungle like no other. It was filled with underground tunnels where the roots of 300-metre trees were being severed one by one, gnawed by giant rodents with electric hedge-clippers instead of teeth. And he dreamt of a city. Or a place that had once been a city and that might someday be a city again. At the moment, it seemed to be between phases, like one of those pictures that changes shape depending which way you tilt it. And finally he dreamt of jungle and city together, speeding toward some sort of denouement that was beyond him, that gave him a headache just thinking about it.

In the morning, Robert awoke with a start – as if someone or something had brushed his face gently to warn him. And a warning was exactly what it had been. He scrambled out of the greenhouse a few steps ahead of the city employee whose job it was to make sure the temperature controls functioned properly. Perhaps, there was no need for such haste, Robert thought, once he was outside and looking across a frozen river from which the mist rose like dirty dry ice. Perhaps, the employee might have greeted him with a pleasant: "Hello, friend." And: "Would you like to share a cup of java?"

Perhaps. But Robert couldn't take the chance. The last public service employee he'd encountered had kicked him squarely in the chest as he lay on a heating grill just inside one of the city's subway stations. The insulation was the only thing that saved him from broken ribs and slow death from internal bleeding. So, without a second thought, he had bid his steamy paradise farewell and hurled himself into the cold, barely managing to pull the panel up behind him.

"That's the end of that," he told himself, feeling the sharp cold bite at his lungs. "But who cares, eh? *'Among so many people cozy in their homes/I am like a man who explores far-off oceans./Days with full stomachs stand on their tables;/I see a distant land full of images.'* Now, where the hell did I get that tidbit from? Ah, of course. 'The Solitary Person,' Rainer Maria Rilke. One of my very favourites."

The words, coming to him on their own, uninvited, were like glimpses of another time. For Robert the Hobo had once been Robert the High School English Teacher – when such things still existed or mattered. And his head was full of similar nonsense, snatches of verses for every occasion. Or none. But this time he was wrong. It wasn't the end of anything. When he returned that night, after a day spent at the bottom of a subway station escalator, hand thrust out and hoping against hope, he fell through the same panel into the same greenhouse.

"They missed it! Goddammit, they missed it! I don't know how – and I don't care – but they did."

He rubbed his hands with glee as he replaced the panel for the second time. It was only after he'd removed his coat and settled down for another miraculous night that he noticed a small form by his feet. At first, it seemed inert. But then it began to shudder, as if it couldn't control its own movements. Boot in hand, ready to strike in case of attack, Robert leaned over to get a better look. And then quickly lowered his boot.

"Sweet Jesus. How did you get here?"

It was a puppy. Soon to be *his* puppy, his No-Name Puppy. A ragged mop with floppy ears and enormous eyes that practically glowed in the dark. But there's no need to describe it in detail, is there? Anyone who wishes may still see it (if they hurry, that is), immortalized for future generations in the nearby park. At the time, it was still unaware of its destiny, still unsure of what would come next. So the tiny creature cowered as Robert brought his hand down to pet it. Then, realizing the man meant no harm, it reached up to lick his fingers.

Robert and the puppy slept side by side that night, the puppy snuggled against the man's chest, trying to get at his nipple. There were more dreams for Robert. They made, if possible, less sense than the ones from the previous night. And it seemed, the several times Robert awoke after a particularly vivid one, that even the puppy whimpered convulsively.

In the morning, Robert was startled awake by the sound of an unearthly yelp. What he saw had him rubbing his eyes in disbelief. There, suspended above him and being slowly pulled up into the sky, was the puppy. It struggled and cried in the grasp of one of the vines; it released a stream of urine; it defecated mightily. But nothing helped. Up the poor, frightened, shit-encrusted creature went, up toward the maw of a darkly foliated plant that had no nameplate. Robert envisioned the bones being spit out one at a time. Or perhaps dissolved in corrosive acid that effectively reversed the roles of predator and prey.

"No!" Robert the Hobo screamed and at the same time realized the futility of his gesture. How could screaming at a plant – albeit a carnivorous one – produce results?

But it seemed to. The vine hesitated, quivering, rocking back and forth. It held the puppy just beyond reach for a moment – as if weighing it. Then gently let it down. The second the puppy hit solid ground, it scrambled to hide behind Robert's leg and let off several volleys of barking before another feint from the vine made it go mute. The vine hovered above Robert's head, weaving about like a snake.

Robert could sense, however, that this was no "ordinary" carnivorous plant and that it meant him no harm. Or rather that the word "harm" didn't exist in its vocabulary. It reached down and, before he had a chance to react, stuck a sucker to his temple. Immediately, he had the same visions as the two nights gone by. Only now he knew they weren't dreams, at least not the kind met in sleep. And the images, crystal clear and sharply focused, made complete sense to him. Though he fervently wished some of them might not.

"You're the human we've been looking for," came the voice inside his head, mercifully clearing away the images before they became unbearable – like trapped sheets of lightning, flashing back and forth, ever increasing in amplitude till… till the necessary explosion, the smell of burnt bark. Or sizzling, totally fried neurons.

Amid the puzzlement, the frazzled scramble to understand, Robert knew one thing: this was definitely not his own voice, not that internal orator reciting fragments of favourite rhymes or carrying on imaginary conversations with people who didn't even speak his language. For one thing, it was soft, feminine, when such differences were still being observed.

"What do you want with me?" he said, a split second before his mouth actually formed the question. Telepathy. That was it. He had heard of that.

"You know that already, don't you? What is the meaning of those words we find in your head: *'The tulips are too excitable, it is winter here./Look how white everything is, how quiet, how snowed-in./I am learning peacefulness, lying by myself quietly /As the light lies on these white walls, this bed, these hands.'*?"

142

"'I am nobody; I have nothing to do with explosions','" Robert said, continuing the verses. "It's from a poem. Something called 'Tulips' by an ancient poet named Sylvia Plath."

"Yes, we know that," the vines said, waving as if impatiently. "But what do they mean? What's their significance?"

"Significance?" Robert creased his brow. "You wouldn't understand. It's a poem – from a time of intense neurosis. You have to be human to understand it. Besides, there aren't poems or neuroses anymore so there's no chance of understanding now – even if you were human."

"Ah, we see now. *And I have no face, I have wanted to efface myself./The vivid tulips eat my oxygen.*' Death. They have to do with death. Death we understand very well. A yanking, is it not? An unimaginable snipping away? A loss of contact with the good earth itself? The ultimate unrooting? Precisely what is happening at this very moment."

They *did* understand. Robert the Hobo suddenly felt very tired, as if he were being drained of some essential fluid. Or pulled down by gravity. His arms fell by his sides; his legs were rubber beneath him. He didn't know how he was still standing, what was holding him up.

"We're sorry," the voices said, obviously reading his thoughts. "We didn't realize how quickly your species tires. Must be all the effort you put into individuation. And external armour. Very impressive armour, we must add."

The vine just as suddenly released him. He fell head first to the ground, his face in the warm loam. From where he was lying, he saw another tentacle make its way toward the wall panel. Robert knew now he had gone crazy, had definitely gone over the edge. For wasn't that the vine carrying a screwdriver, one of those with interchangeable heads? And not only carrying it but seeming to know what to do with it, which one to use. Yes, the men in the white coats would come soon and take him away. The hospital was quite close. At least it would be warm in there and the porridge, he'd heard, was excellent. If he made enough of a fuss, they might even put him in an isolation ward. That would be exquisite. No one to talk to but himself. The vine pressed the screwdriver against the panel and removed the screws. Then it pulled the panel away from the wall. The cold air revived Robert somewhat.

"You must leave now as the workers are coming. But make sure to return this evening. We'll send the puppy with you as a reminder. Goodbye."

Robert the Hobo stumbled out, hopping about in the snow as he dressed and slipped his boots on one at a time. The panel was immediately replaced behind him – and just as quickly screwed back in. Robert remained standing in the same spot for several minutes. Inside, he could see the day's first worker going about his job. The man, wearing dirty brown overalls, was whistling. He checked the thermostat right beneath the plant that had just recently communicated with Robert, had asked him about poetry and death, no less. Robert didn't know very much about plants but this one looked quite ordinary to him: a thick central stalk several metres high from which issued, at various levels, tentacles of leafy vines. Nothing unusual or frightening about it – no sticky maw, no thought projection, no display of manual dexterity. Everything seemed normal – except perhaps for the fact it had no nameplate.

Robert spent the day – or as much as there was of it – in the public library researching carnivorous plants. He was thankful the facility had been abandoned and sealed up long before as no one actually borrowed or read manuscripts any longer. He recalled vividly the days spent in crowded public libraries, hundreds of humans on all sides of him, beside him, above and below him – and how uncomfortable he had found it to be among so many people in such an enclosed space.

He shuddered. The memory brought back all the reasons why he had taken to the road in the first place – the claustrophobia, the xenophobia, the misanthropy that had plagued him even when he was in the classroom teaching, standing in front of 30 boisterous, hyperactive and ultimately uncaring teenagers who wanted nothing more than to slip a whoopee cushion under his seat. And he remembered very well the day he finally broke down, viciously attacking a pretty high school senior in a cashmere sweater who'd innocently asked him why they didn't study Leonard Cohen (a poetaster of the late 20th century who became popular after he abandoned poetry for song jingles). That had been followed by psychiatric tests, discovery of deep unresolved emotional problems, threats from irate parents and finally, a resignation one step ahead of outright dismissal.

But there was no one else in this public library – except for his puppy, of course, busy marking his territory. The walls of the monumental building were being forced apart by the ebb and flow of ice, the successive thawings and freezings. The ceiling leaked brown water where the pipes had burst. One more winter and the huge marble blocks of its central stairway would come tumbling down in a heap. Inside, the books, those that hadn't been chewed by rats or scavenged for rolling papers, now flowered with icy mould.

Room after room in democratic disarray: Aristotle coupled with Jacqueline Susann; *Psycho-Cybernetics: Updated and Expanded* rubbing spines with *The Classless Society*; Bibles and Korans too close for comfort. Still, after several hours of searching through the rubble, Robert was able to find what he was looking for – a book on the carnivores of the plant world. But it didn't help him much. The largest carnivorous plant yet discovered was something called the *Sarracenia flava 'Maxima'* or Trumpet Pitcher which rose to a height of one metre. The biggest things it could capture were bluebottle flies and wasps which had once made it popular with housewives concerned about damage to the environment from insect repellents.

Besides, it had no tentacles or vines to hold its prey. Instead, it relied on luring the insects down its throat with nectar till they were in too deep to escape. Like marriage, Robert thought, smiling. Or, come to think of it, like any relationship with another human being. This was definitely not the plant at the greenhouse. In fact, search as he might through the volumes on botany, he could find nothing resembling that plant. Maybe it wasn't so ordinary after all.

"A hybrid, of course!" Robert exclaimed. "These mad scientists are always creating hybrids these days. New ones all the time. A secret experiment being conducted by the government – and I've stumbled on to it. They're teaching plant life how to communicate with humans and how to use screwdrivers. In preparation for advanced jungle warfare. No more defoliation. All you do is make the plants your allies and let them attack the enemy for you. Isn't that so, puppy?"

The puppy let off chewing and wagged its tail.

"If that were so," the quiet voice inside Robert said, "then why did the plant let you in on the secret? And where's the security that would normally surround such a project? They'd be using atomic minefields to keep people away."

Robert couldn't shake the distinct feeling the voice was coming from the puppy.

"Naw, it can't be," he said, shaking his head while staring into the puppy's opaque eyes. "Not telepathic dogs, too."

"You're right. I'm not a telepathic dog. I'm part of the same organism you left behind at the greenhouse. And it's about time you headed home to us, don't you think? There's lots of work to do before you're ready – and time presses."

"Before I'm ready for what?"

"Before you're ready to save the world, of course."

"Save the world?" Robert said, his laughter echoing in the huge room. "What, are you nuts or something?"

"Nuts? No, we believe nuts belong to an entirely different family of plants altogether."

"Well, good for them," Robert said, standing up and turning away in the hope of breaking contact. "But you're not getting me anywhere near that place again. No sir. I'd rather take my chances in the middle of a gender-identity lawyers' convention. Or riding the subway at rush hour with a bunch of Jesus freak muckers."

"You were given a choice," the voice said as the puppy followed at his heels. "And the opportunity to back out. But you've already made your decision. It's too late to go back on it now. We're very sorry."

"Oh, it's too late, is it?" Robert said, hoping the sarcasm was dripping through from his head to theirs. "Just watch me – and then we'll see who's sorry."

But watching Robert at that moment would have been a very painful experience. He collapsed suddenly to the marble-veined floor clutching his head. Rather, clawing at it would be a more apt description – as if trying to pull something out of it. Then he began to writhe in a circle, using his head as a pivot and all the while screaming "No!" over and over again till the library was filled with his voice, echoing back and forth with his howls. Finally, he lay there moaning, his tongue darting convulsively in and out of his mouth.

Robert never told anyone what he saw or felt or experienced during those few excruciating seconds. Some say it was a vision of the end of the world so ghastly it turned his eyeballs inside out; others proclaim it a sight of such exquisite spiritual beauty it broke his heart and vaporised his soul. Whatever it was, Robert arose from his trance a different man. And he followed quietly, zombie-like, as the puppy pranced and capered his way back to the greenhouse in the middle of the winter's worst snowstorm.

Once inside again, Robert sat down cross-legged directly in front of the plant – and didn't even flinch when the tentacle slithered through the air and attached itself with a "suck-a-suck" to the side of his head.

"Hello, Bob," the voice said, the epitome of gentleness. "You don't mind if I call you Bob, do you?" Bob shook his head. "Good. Bob's a nice name, isn't it? You can even say it backwards without anyone noticing the difference. Unlike 'God' or 'metonymy'. You're probably saying to yourself right about now: 'What the hell do they want with me?' That is what you're thinking, no?" Bob nodded. "Well, as a matter of fact, we do want you for something, something of extreme importance, something which is only possible at this particular time and at no other. You see, Bob, we need you to help save the Earth. Your days as an outcast and renegade are definitely numbered. Soon, you'll be by far the most important member of the entire human race with responsibilities that would crush you if you had to bear them alone. Fortunately, we're here to lend support. We've been empowered, mandated, to bring it about. And we can't afford to miss the opportunity for our time is limited and it might never come again. Together, we'll try to undo the harm that's been perpetrated; we'll labour to repair the wounds; we'll seal up the pus-infested sores; we'll restore the Earth to its pristine beauty. Forever and ever. Let us show you how."

Bob, no longer a hobo but not quite a preacher either, toppled over on his side and slept. He slept throughout the rest of the winter. Not once did he move, not even to twitch an eyebrow or shake a leg. In fact, a sort of greenish cocoon grew around him where he lay. By some chemistry unknown to human science, the puppy performed all Bob's physical functions for him: the eating, drinking and defecating mostly, but also the exercising to keep his limbs from atrophying and the general observation of the outside world. And the workers going about their daily rounds in the greenhouse not once noticed the mound of green, cottony substance at the foot of the unnamed plant. It was as if a shield of non-being had been set in place to protect him from prying eyes. Whatever it may have been, Bob wasn't once disturbed as the winds continued to howl and the snow piled high against the very panel that had opened to let him in – now very securely in pláce.

It must have been the renewed heat and vigour of the spring sun that finally made Bob stir. He sat up and pulled away the material around him. His puppy tried to help as well but, even though it yanked for all it was worth, it managed only to get itself more and more entangled till it ended up chasing its own tail and barking madly. Bob laughed and stood up, stretching, his fingers arching upwards as far as they could go. He began to sing, to hum.

"Hey, what's going on in there?" a voice called out from one of the other sections. "There's not supposed to be—"

As the worker in his dirty brown overalls walked through the door, there was a sudden constriction in his throat. No matter how much he tried, he couldn't get another word out. It was all he could do to stand there in the doorway, staring at Bob the Preacher and his No-Name Puppy like they were apparitions from another world. In fact, Bob looked no different than the first night he had stumbled onto the greenhouse. A little scruffier, perhaps, and threadbare – but that was it. Nothing had changed in his physical appearance that would cause such a reaction in the worker. And he still wore his insulated coat and seven league boots, with the greasy toque pulled low over his forehead.

Bob put his hand on the worker's shoulder as he went by him. Friendly and always smiling – that was Bob the Preacher's way. Even when his message wasn't all that pleasant. Even when it was downright unpalatable. And it usually worked, too – at least for those who allowed themselves to be touched. The worker relaxed visibly and returned Bob's smile.

"May I offer you a cup of coffee?" he asked on regaining his voice. Bob shook his head. "Ah, yes. You're in a hurry?" Bob nodded. "Let me show you the way out then." He led Bob and the puppy to the front entrance of the greenhouse. "Here we are. It's a beautiful morning, isn't it?" And indeed it was – despite the deformed fish floating belly-up along the river's edge and the smog masks that obscured many of the joggers' faces.

"Have a pleasant day. And come back soon, you hear. I make a fresh pot every day."

Not everyone, of course, reacted in the same way when they encountered Bob the Preacher and his puppy strolling down the riverfront path. Some wanted to come closer, to touch his rags; others recoiled as if in disgust. Women, in particular, steered clear of him – especially those who were of child-bearing age. Bob himself didn't seem to notice either reaction and continued to walk in a leisurely fashion, soaking in the sun and occasionally discarding pieces of his clothing. Only the sound of an explosion behind him caused him to stop for a moment and turn around. What he saw was the top of the greenhouse flying through the air; steel, and glass shooting in all directions, as the plants broke out of their imprisonment.

"Ah, now we can breathe," the voice in his head said. "It's springtime for the Earth."

Several of the people who happened to be close to the building when it exploded could now be seen lying on the ground speared by slivers of glass. But that was no concern of Bob's. There were more important things to do. He was standing next to a shredded maple tree that was struggling to survive in the middle of a gigantic blacktop parking lot. This was where the joggers left their vehicles before hitting the riverfront paths for their morning exercise. It wasn't so much a tree actually as a grouping of bare branches about the height of a man. The branches, where they hadn't been snapped by children, ravaged by ice or scorched by car exhaust fumes, were covered with a thin layer of soot. In other words, a tree not even fit for insects to gnaw on.

After gently brushing away the soot, Bob found one or two buds, just tiny bumps really against the bark. But it meant the tree was alive – if only barely. Bob placed his hand on the living branch, feeling the feeble pulse, the shrivelled roots sucking away at PCB-enriched nourishment. Suddenly, the tree shot into the air, zooming up 20 metres or more without hesitation. Its trunk thickened to two metres in diameter. A dense canopy of leaves arched out in a perfectly symmetrical circle with a radius of 10 metres. From its base, the ground undulated, the asphalt cracked open, shaking off the parked cars like ants and hurling some into the river before covering the entire area with a thick, undulating carpet of dandelions and chicory plants.

The whole time Bob and his puppy stood beneath it, either unaware of or ignoring the screams of those who had witnessed the transformation. And, just as swiftly as it had begun, it was over. Now, there was absolute silence, perhaps for the first time ever – but definitely not the last. Birds alighted in the branches without the least chirp; squirrels ran up the trunk on tiptoe; a fish leaped out of the water for a glass-eyed look – and noise-lessly re-entered.

Humans started to gather around, though making sure to stay well outside the perimeter of the maple's shade, which somehow always remained a perfectly symmetrical circle no matter where the sun happened to be. Bob put his hand on the trunk, fingertips on bark. As he made contact, his voice rang out for all to hear – and yet no one in the steadily thickening crowd once saw him open his mouth.

"My name is Bob the Preacher," he said in his awful, silent way. "Heed my words if you wish to save the Earth from total annihilation. I am not the saviour, no. I'm just a poor hobo. But I can show you how *you* can save the Earth before it's too late. Heed my words. There are powerful forces behind me. They're angry at what you've done, at the destruction you've set in motion in so short a stewardship. But they're willing to give you a chance to set it right, to save yourselves. They also know that you don't believe something just because someone tells you so. So they're willing to give you a sample of their terrible power. Watch the news tonight and you'll see what I mean. Thank you."

With that the voice stopped. And the spell was broken. Suddenly, the silence was replaced by the sound of sirens and the screeching of tires. Policemen with cattle prods ordered the crowd to disperse. One of them, a bulked-up young man wearing an opaque visor, approached Bob the Preacher with the obvious intention of arresting him for disturbing the peace.

"Hey, you," he said. "What do you think you're doing? Public speaking without a permit is strictly against the law. Sorry, but I'm gonna have to take you in."

But, the moment he tried to pass the line between shadow and light, he was sent bouncing back, reeling to the ground.

"Shit!" he said, holding his bloodied nose.

"I'm sorry," the voice said. "You can't enter. It's forbidden for humans to enter the area reserved for Bob the Preacher and his No-Name Puppy."

"What the fuck you talking about, scumbag!" The policeman yelled. "I'll enter where the fuck I want." But the policeman's second attempt to penetrate the tree's canopy was just as unsuccessful as the first. At this point, he unholstered his gun and aimed it at the scabby-looking vagabond's head. "Come out, asshole – and be quick about it. Otherwise, I'll wipe that fucking smile off your face for good."

"The News at Six," the voice said, ignoring the policeman. "Tune into the news."

The policeman fired. Fortunately for him, the ricocheting bullet whizzed right by his head. One of the bystanders, a young mother pushing a baby carriage, wasn't so lucky. She dropped to the ground in a pool of blood, clutching at her chest as the carriage continued across the street on its own.

"Please don't fire again," the voice said. "You might injure someone else."

"Don't you fucking try to tell me what to fucking do!" the policeman shouted, the gun shaking in his hand as his face flamed red. "You're in no position to give orders. Now, either you come out of there this instant or I call the riot squad – and those motherfuckers will blow you to kingdom come before you can stick a thumb up your stinking arse."

The policeman was true to his word. The riot squad came, grim, death-masked, bristling with the latest crowd control weaponry and AI-guided armaments. And, cutting a swath through the citizenry, they surrounded the tree, formed *un cordon sanitaire* around it, as much to keep the surging crowds away as to prevent Bob the Preacher from escaping. But Bob had no intention of fleeing. He just sat beneath the tree, waiting. Those looking on saw only a middle-aged man dressed in rags and, next to him, his even scruffier dog. What they didn't realize was that he was in constant communion with his spirits and knew, minute by minute, what was going on throughout the world.

"The news you have been waiting so anxiously for has arrived," the voice said to the crowd at precisely 6 p.m. "See it for yourselves."

No one needed a TV screen for this news. First, there was the image of a woman, an announcer, all out of breath. She could hardly speak for her excitement, hardly get the words out:

"Toronto is a calm city tonight. After more than 100 years of constant shelling, the rockets, the mortars, the sub-machine guns are quiet. How is this possible? How did it happen? No one knows. The various leaders are in emergency session at this very moment, refusing to answer any questions."

This was followed by scenes of the city itself, mostly rubble by now, and the surrounding area. It was a sight to make arms manufacturers and dealers head for the nearest high-rise window. It seemed that every rocket launcher, every bazooka and mortar battery, every machine gun, rifle and pistol had been encircled by vines. Soldiers, rebels, snipers could barely take aim before a vine sprang up and seized their weapons. And it was no use trying to hack them free. Those hacking, stabbing, slicing weapons were immobilized as well.

Slowly, right before the very eyes of the world, Toronto was restored to its former glory. Every trace of the civil war was erased in a matter of minutes as the buildings rose from the dust, the roads repaired themselves and the streetlights came to life. No, it wasn't just restored to its former glory. In the days to come, it became an even more beautiful city, a veritable garden where life's struggle no longer concerned the inhabitants. And there were trees and shrubs everywhere, the air thick with the fragrance of flowers and fruits. It was as if the people of Toronto were being rewarded for the years of misery; the decades of living like frightened rats in tunnels beneath the ground.

But, even if the puzzled natives of the city were more than pleased with the sudden upturn in their fortunes, the sentiment was in no way universal. Already, in various capitals around the world, there were rumblings of a deep conspiracy. While politicians and military leaders pointed fingers and thumped bargaining tables; scientists went about proclaiming the impossibility of such an event; how it went against all the laws of nature; how energy couldn't just be created out of nothing; how entropy had to be served and couldn't be so arbitrarily reversed.

And then some of them – not scientists really but ad executives experienced in such things – quickly came up with a theory. Mass hypnosis, the same phenomenon that had brought them Nazi America. Even you, my sisters and brothers, have heard of Nazi America. It's in all the books. In any case, their theory was that Toronto hadn't changed at all – only people's perception of it. The same with the man sitting under a maple tree. All we have to do, the ad exec-scientists explained, is ignore it and go about our business. After all, illusions can only hurt if you believe them. And, though some felt in their hearts that the theory was flawed in some way, that's what most of the humans did, blithely bypassing Bob the Preacher and Toronto, the city that could have been a splendid tribute to a new consciousness.

"These humans are ingenious in their ingenuousness," the voices said. "They have as much inner armour as outer. It's time we show them that we mean business."

"Business?" Bob the Preacher said, feeling a bit queasy, especially after his puppy howled and tried to bury its head. "What do you mean by that?"

"Yes. It's time to give them a taste of what we can really do. Tell us, Bob. You, as a former human, should know. Where are the worst atrocities being committed in the world today?"

Bob fidgeted. He felt somewhat like a traitor, a quisling. Besides, there were so many atrocities, injustices and both natural and unnatural disasters he really didn't know where to start: Indigenous Peoples on display in cages around the world, the poor and inner city homeless being deliberately culled and marked for elimination, scions of the utterly wealthy kidnapping asexuals for their off-Earth orgies.

"Well," he said at last. "You've got your choice really. Just about anywhere but Toronto right now."

"Hmm," the voices said thoughtfully. "Those are all good, all worthy of redress. But it's not quite what we want."

"I was reading a magazine—"

"Yes!" the voices exclaimed, trembling with excitement. "We have it! That's it! Off you go."

And, as they said that, Bob the Preacher found himself not sitting quietly beneath a maple tree but scrambling up the side of an excavation in a torrential rain, loaded down with a sack full of crushed rocks and desperately trying to pull himself up a rickety rope ladder. He paused to look around. There were thousands of others in the pit with him, all covered in thick mud. Some were scaling the ladders that seemed never-ending in the mist; others were several hundred metres below, rushing about at the bottom of the pit. And this wasn't the only pit. The vast area was pockmarked with them, like giant pus-holes on the face of the Earth.

He could see that not all the men would make it out of those pits alive, that some had already drowned or been crushed beneath the weight of their loads. A whip cracked above his head and there were shouts for him to move along. With the last of his strength, he managed to climb over the top of the pit. There, a man in a yellow slicker immediately pointed a gun at him and directed him to a pile of well-guarded earth where he was told to dump his load. Some of the earth glittered as he spilled it out of his sack. High above, a man with a gold pinkie ring floated over the ground in a covered sedan chair. Bob made his way back to the pit. As he slowly descended the ladder, he spoke to the others, to the thousands who laboured away – not just in this pit but in all of them at once.

"You are destroying me," his voice said, in a tone that forced them to lay down their picks and listen. "You are cutting me to pieces – and for what? For earth that glitters. You are digging away the foundations, tearing out the roots. My trees are sinking into oblivion. Their giant carcasses rotting in your acid rain. The waters… the polluted waters are rolling in… flooding… drowning in carbon dioxide. My forest has run out of air to breathe. It can no longer feed its million billion mouths. But no more. It has gone too far. Lay down your picks for good. Abandon your futile labours. Walk away now. Or suffer the consequences."

But even as he said it, Bob knew that the listening was only temporary. Oh, one or two of the men did have the nerve to walk away – but they were quickly gunned down and their bodies tossed back into the pit. The rest looked at one another for a moment – and then, at the crack of a whip, returned to work. Bob found himself back beneath his maple tree. He was crying and his puppy was licking his face, doing its best to comfort him, to convince him that what was about to happen was necessary.

"Let me try again," Bob pleaded, ever the kind-hearted preacher. "I know I can get them to listen. Please. Deep down, these are good people."

The voices didn't answer. Instead, bodies began to pop up in the grass around the tree. Partly buried in the ground, only their heads and shoulders showing, these bodies were nevertheless still alive – for the moment. Some were screaming in awful torment as their skulls were emptied by ever-busy insects, leaving the tongues for last. Others never got over the shock and died in silence, using their last moments to reflect on what might have been. In an effort to save them, policemen and paramedics ran about the grass trying to pull them out of the ground. Their bodies came away in pieces. So, when saving them didn't work, the police tried to put a quick end to their misery. They shot them, crushed their heads like rotten watermelons, ran them over with their cars and paddy wagons.

At the start of the carnage, Bob the Preacher had lowered his eyes. But that hadn't kept him from witnessing every last bit of it, reflected inside his head. He even recognized some of the bodies – especially one in a yellow slicker and another who, before being devoured alive by centipedes, disgorged a gold pinkie ring.

"*I didn't want any flowers, I only wanted / To lie with my hands turned up and be utterly empty.*"

"That's no longer possible," the voices said. "We must prove that what we do is no illusion."

In a matter of minutes, the thousands of bodies had started to decompose. The stench was awful, driving away even the hardiest spectator. Many of the riot policemen, ordered to remain at their posts, fainted despite their gas masks. The stench rose as a cloud and settled over the city. It penetrated to the very pores. There was no escaping it, leaving the inhabitants to hang over their toilet bowls.

Later that very same day, someone in authority stood before Bob the Preacher. She wore an asbestos and anti-radiation suit and talked through a loudspeaker.

"Who are you?" she asked in a forceful way designed to get answers. "What do you want from us?"

"I'm Bob the Preacher. I'm here to save the Earth – if you'll let me. Have you the authority—"

"You call this saving the Earth?" she said, her face twisting. "It's murder – pure and simple."

"Some must die so that others can live. Today, the rain forest is healthy again. The mines have been filled in. The trees are upright, their roots reaching deep into the earth, secure. There is peace."

"What bloody well gives you the right to decide when peace comes or not?" She stabbed her finger repeatedly toward him. "Were you elected?"

"Elected? Is that what you call it? The elected ones? Perhaps, so. A long time ago."

"Well, let me tell you something, buster. You weren't elected by me. Or by anyone else around here. We run a democratic system in this country. So no one tells us what to do. Neither you nor your Arab dictator friends. They're behind all this, aren't they? I should've known. They're the only ones with the money. What do they want? A monopoly on the world's energy."

"We are democratic, too. Our 'Arab dictator friends' were given neither more nor less than you – just an equal portion of the bodies. After all, they're just as guilty."

"Guilty! Of course, they're guilty. But what's that got to do with us?"

"This is fruitless. You humans have a well-honed penchant for blaming others for your problems. Passing the buck, I believe you call it."

"I'll show you what we have a penchant for, you shit-corroded pile of rags!" she screamed. "If you don't come out from under that tree within the hour, we're going to hit you with everything we got. Everything! Do you understand? And let me tell you I damn well have the authority."

The woman in authority meant what she said. When Bob the Preacher hadn't emerged in the allotted time, the heavy-duty lasers moved in. Crackling with blue lightning, they raked him and the tree full blast: from above, from straight ahead and from below. Not one ray got through. Then, after a 15-minute warning to the residents, they dropped a low-level radiation device that destroyed a good portion of that part of the city and the surrounding countryside, leaving dark shadows against any of the buildings that still stood.

But Bob the Preacher, his puppy, the tree, and its shadow remained untouched. Finally, they hit it with their most powerful fusion bomb, as yet untested under actual conditions of war. The island vanished, the rivers around it dried up, the sky turned black, radiation poisoning spread over a radius of several hundred kilometres. Still the little green oasis floated, unharmed in the midst of so much destruction. Even then, however, the humans didn't give up. They continued to drop bomb after bomb on it, hoping to deplete its energy supply, to find the weakness in it, the fatal flaw. For they knew nothing that didn't have some flaw; a way for entropy to sneak in.

"These humans are a tenacious bunch," the voices said with what seemed a hint of admiration. "It almost makes you want to leave them be on their path to absolute destruction, let them fall off the edge, dragging everything else with them. But we can't do that, can we? Wait a minute! Perhaps if we give them a little taste of it, just a tiny feel for that total annihilation, they might finally relent, might finally admit the *mea culpa* of their actions. Bob, it's time to do your duty again. Sound the warning. Let them know we too mean business."

Amid the almost constant thunderclap of atomic bombs and the remote-controlled robotic devices hurling themselves with preprogrammed ferocity against the tree, Bob spoke out once again. This time, however, his voice was weary and the sadness in it was unmistakable.

"Humans," he said, the voice, though it quavered and faltered, penetrating to the very depths of their fallout shelters, to the bored-out mountains, to the ever-circling shark-nosed submarines, to the insect-like drones. "I'm to inform you that the Earth is ready to withdraw its bounty from you, to buck you off its broad back. It has fed and nourished you faithfully until now even while you were stabbing it repeatedly, even while you were tearing out her very womb. It has supported every atrocity, every act of violence and, each time, it has come back stronger than ever, with renewed vigour. But this is it. No more. Nada. Let us demonstrate."

And with that, every blade of grass, every stalk of corn, every sheath of grain, every vine, every bush, and every tree – every tree but one, that is – vanished from the face of the Earth. Just as the bodies had come shooting out, the plants slipped in. Gone, disappeared without a trace. It was a scene that should make us shudder to this day, so many lifetimes removed even those who keep track have lost track. No desert could be so desolate and cold; no lifeless moon so barren; no polished skull so empty.

"Until you come to your senses," the voice said, "this is the way it shall be. We are sure it won't be long though. At least, we hope not."

For a while, it seemed the voices were right. Not long after the Earth withdrew its bounty, the leaders of the humans called for a truce – and talks. They were willing to discuss the conditions laid down.

"Ah," the voices said to Bob, "this must make you exceedingly glad. We will have peace at last."

For the first time in a very long time Bob allowed himself a smile, albeit a tiny one. His faith in the human ability to adapt had nearly vanished during that period. Now, they were finally coming to their senses.

"We have chosen you to conduct the talks for us," the voices told him. "A team of human negotiators will be flown in presently. We will not ask for much – just a sharing of the Earth among equals. We don't want slaves, just as humans don't want to be slaves. We want only continuity."

The team of human negotiators consisted of three. Among them – nay, leading them – Bob recognized the woman in authority, the one who had threatened him and had ordered the unleashing of so much death and destruction. Now, she came wearing her diplomatic peace cap and carrying a bouquet of artificial flowers in her hands.

"Greetings," Bob said, as he lowered the energy shield around the tree to allow them in. "It's a pleasure to see that humans haven't lost their age-old instinct for survival. And that they're still capable of solving problems in a peaceful way. Now, where shall we begin?"

"By getting rid of you!" the woman screamed.

And she yanked one of the fake flowers, blowing herself and everyone within a kilometre radius sky high. Everyone, that is, except Bob, his No-Name Puppy, and the tree. All three came floating gently back to Earth – or whatever was left of it.

"That does it," the voices said. "When we're through with them, they'll come crawling to us. They'll be willing to do anything. They'll volunteer to be our pets, to clean out our intestines, to inhabit the recesses of our anal tracts."

But, one more time, the voices hadn't anticipated, hadn't counted on, the stubbornness – and never-say-die resourcefulness – of the human animal. In the midst of mass starvation and turmoil, in the midst of general cannibalism and slaughter, of diaspora and social collapse, some survived. They survived by producing food through genetic manipulation, by imitating the very plants themselves in their high-tech labs. Vegetation was created out of desktops, out of the decomposing bodies of the less fortunate, out of shoestrings and hockey sticks. Everything that could be converted to food was – for those with the means to pay for it.

"This is ridiculous," the voices said in exasperation. "Bob, we don't know what to do. Instead of admitting they were wrong, instead of trying a new way, a way that would be best for all of us, these humans would rather fight to the death. They would rather pile up their dead in our path, their billions upon billions slaughtered – and for what reason? Is what we offer them so bad? No, they want dominion or nothing. What are we going to do, Bob? Look, they're mocking us. They're hiding behind their armour. Aren't they a pretty sight? Bob, what would you have us do?"

But Bob the Preacher wasn't listening. Bob was crying. He was in mourning for his species, for all the innocents that had been destroyed and for the many more yet to come; for those who would have envisioned a different world if only they'd been given the chance; and for those who were stubborn and proud and stupid enough to hold out until the end – even if they knew they were wrong. He was also in mourning because he realized there was nothing more he could do. The decision had already been made and their fate sealed. The genetically engineered food would turn to poison in their mouths – and they would fall by the wayside, each and every last one of them, their faces like death masks pressed against the vacuum-sealed glass. Then the Earth would be meticulously reconstructed – the jungles, the rivers, the mountains; the greenhouses, the jogging paths, the public libraries; the timber wolves, the puppies, the insects. Well, maybe not the public libraries and jogging paths!

"And a few humans," Bob said, with a hint of hope. "Don't forget a few human beings. After all, they created the cities and the books. They're not all bad, you know. Besides, they would be a great way to top off your rebuilt world, wouldn't they? Admit it. They're the finest thing in all of creation, the crowning glory."

"If they can't live with us," the voices answered reverberating with sternness, with a collective shaking of their heads, "we are better off without them."

The last scene in this tale takes place on a beach facing one of the Earth's great oceans. The water is warm and silky, teeming with new life. The sun emits exactly the right amount of light and heat, without any dangerous radiation. Lying on the beach, the gentle waves lapping against her legs, is a woman. A young woman wearing nothing but a ratty cashmere sweater. Sitting beside her is Bob the Preacher and his No-Name Puppy. After a few moments, the woman is roused from what seems an ageless sleep.

"Who am I?" she says, yawning, stretching, shading her eyes from the sun.

"You're the last human being on Earth," Bob says aloud, his own voice sounding exceedingly strange to him.

"But that can't be," she says. "Why, look. You're here."

"Not really."

"No," she says, touching his arm. "No riddles. You're a man; I'm a woman. A man and a woman were put on Earth to make children. We must make children. That can't be denied."

"I suppose not," Bob says.

"Then, let's get to it!"

And with that she pulls off his few remaining rags and brings him down on her, lowers him onto her. He does everything a man must do, culminating in a rabid spurting as she wraps her legs around him for better penetration. Afterwards, he rolls away, hiding his face. It's only then that the woman notices something strange between her legs. The water lapping against them, touching the vaginal cavity, is turning a darkly foliated shade of green.

"What's that?" she screams, rubbing herself and waving the green-tinted hand before his eyes. "What have you done to me? What have you filled me with?"

"I told you I wasn't a man. I've filled you with the green fuse of life. That's all I can do."

"You bastard! You fucking traitor! You twisted freak! I don't want any green fuse. I want babies. I want humans to reclaim their rightful place. Right next to the gods. If you can't give me that, then fuck you. May you be cursed for all eternity. May you be remembered down through the ages as the man who did away with human beings, his own flesh and blood."

And, saying that, she grows old and shrivels, weeping for all the children she'll never have. Above her, a rocket trails smoke through the sky, signalling perhaps the end of a species. Or the start of something new.

"'*The water I taste is warm and salt, like the sea,/And comes from a country far away as health.*'"

Bob the Preacher can feel the hard tug within him, the ebb and flow of the blood. He thinks back on that corrosive winter day when it all started, when Robert the Hobo fell through a wall panel into the heat and the vision of a greenhouse where a unique symbiosis took place. At the same time, he can feel the human in him returning and that makes him hurt even more. It manifests itself as a state of confusion that causes him to hold his head – just like that first time when he grovelled on the floor of an abandoned library, hoping one of the marble blocks would detach itself and put him out of his misery. But before he can get too far, before he can reactivate the mechanisms that'll have him back as Robert the Hobo, his lovable, friendly No-Name Puppy jumps on his chest and, wagging its tail excitedly, slits his throat with a razor-sharp nail, neatly from ear to ear.

Since it was my turn for storytelling and since no one's exempt from the duty, I chose the tale of how the Earth was saved from total and utter destruction by Bob the Preacher and his No-Name Puppy – both of whom can be seen at least for the time being, deeply rooted and well-nourished at last, next to the perfectly symmetrical maple.

*Now that The Sleepers have returned and are on the verge of landing at the edge of Forest Earth, I hope the story hasn't caused offence to anyone. I offer it not as an object lesson but as a sign of forgiveness, as a signal that things may turn out differently this time around. And, if they don't, well… There may be those among us who would fault you, Mother, for what they feel is about to befall us, for a renewed uncertainty that may never be set right. There are those who may say you could have prevented it – if you had so wished. That you could have secured our future – and the Earth's – for time immemorial. But who can blame you for feeling pity? Who can blame you for showing mercy? Who can blame you for not destroying every single human being after all, for allowing those pathetic few to escape? No one can fight their own nature, can they, Mother Yggdrasil, Great Tree of Life? No one. Not even you.*

## Acknowledgements

I thank Bruce Meyer for making the selection of stories in this collection, and for his editorial advice.

Some of the stories in this collection have been published previously, if not necessarily in this final form:

"Milk Run" in *Another Realm*
"The Mother" in *Challenging Destiny*
"Paradise Island" in *SpaceWays Weekly*
"Rules of Conduct" in *Tesseracts 2*
"Casebook: In the Matter of Father Dante Lazaro" in
  *Challenging Destiny*